RIDE THE
HARD LAND

Raymond D. Mason

RIDE THE HARD LAND

Copyright © 2012 by Raymond D. Mason

All rights reserved. No part of this book may be used or reproduced by any means, graphic, electronic, or mechanical; including photocopying, recording, taping or by any information storage retrieval system without the written permission of the publisher/author except in the case of brief quotations embodied in critical articles and reviews.

Raymond D. Mason books may be ordered through authorized booksellers associated with Mason Books or by contacting:

You may order books through:
www.CreateSpace.com
www.Target.com
www.Bordersbooks.com
orwww.Amazon.com

or personalized autographed copies from:
E-mail: RMason3092@aol.com

(541) 679-0396

This is a work of fiction. All characters, names, incidents, organizations, and dialogue in this novel are either the products of the author's imagination or are used fictitiously.

Cover by Raymond D. Mason
Printed in the United States of America

Books by This Author

Mysteries

8 Seconds to Glory
A Motive for Murder
A Tale of Tri-Cities
A Walk on the Wilder Side
Beyond Missing
Blossoms in the Dust *
Brotherhood of the Cobra
Corrigan
If Looks Could Kill
Illegal Crossing
In the Chill of the Night
Most Deadly Intentions
Murder on the Oregon Express
Odor In the Court
On a Lonely Mountain Road
Send in the Clones
Shadows of Doubt
Sleazy Come, Sleazy Go
Suddenly, Murder
The Mystery of Myrtle Creek
The Return of 'Booger' Doyle
The Secret of Spirit Mountain
The Tootsie Pop Kid
The Woman in the Field
Too Late To Live

Westerns

Aces and Eights
Across the Rio Grande
Beyond the Great Divide *
Beyond the Picket Wire
Brimstone; End of the Trail
Day of the Rawhiders
Four Corners Woman
Incident at Medicine Bow
King of the Barbary Coast
Laramie
Last of the Long Riders
Night of the Blood Red Moon
Night Riders
Purple Dawn
Rage at Del Rio
Rebel Pride
Return to Cutter's Creek
Ride the Hellfire Trail
Showdown at Lone Pine
Streets of Durango: Lynching
Streets of Durango: Shootings
Tales of Old Arizona
The Long Ride Back
Three Days to Sundown
Yellow Sky, Black Hawk

Raymond D. Mason

TABLE OF CONTENTS

Préface

Chapter 01 :	**Arrival in Sundown**
Chapter 02 :	**The first gunfight**
Chapter 03 :	**Brian comes home**
Chapter 04 :	**Brian tells AJ about Brent**
Chapter 05 :	**Nugent's and the Rangers**
Chapter 06 :	**Chauncey and the gambler**
Chapter 07 :	**Brent awakes in Sundown**
Chapter 08 :	**Arrival at Possum Creek**
Chapter 09 :	**The stagecoach holdup**
Chapter 10 :	**An accidental shooting**
Chapter 11 :	**Brent returns to Sundown**
Chapter 12 :	**Chauncey goes too far**
Chapter 13 :	**The brothers ride out**
Chapter 14:	**Four Fingers escapes**
Chapter 15:	**Heading for Sundown**
Chapter 16:	**Haggerty and Jordan**
Chapter 17:	**Hello Lincoln Sackett**
Chapter 18:	**Arrival in Sundown**
Chapter 19:	**The Rangers come calling**
Chapter 20:	**The Reunion**

PREFACE

BRIAN SACKETT left home in pursuit of a man he thought had tried to kill his brother, A.J. The man who claimed to be an eyewitness to the shooting turned out to be the actual shooter. Because the truth was uncovered after Brian had already set out in pursuit of the man falsely accused; there was no way of informing him that he was pursuing an innocent man.

Along the way Brian discovered that Brent, his identical twin brother, who the family believed had been killed in the War Between the States, was actually alive and on the run from the law. The two brothers met in San Antonio when their paths crossed by accident. It was a short, bittersweet reunion.

Brian eventually caught up with the man he'd been pursuing in Laredo, Texas; it was there that he learned the man was dead; he had been killed by the Laredo sheriff. Brian headed back to Abilene looking forward to getting back to work on the ranch.

He wished that Brent could one day return to the family ranch, but figured it to be highly unlikely with Brent being a man on the dodge. Still, he could hope.

JULIA SUMMERS and her husband, along with his brother, his brother's wife, and a friend, were on their way to Sundown, Texas where they had purchased a small ranch. While crossing open range they were attacked by ranch hands who worked for a ruthless rancher. Julia's husband and the others were killed, but Julia survived.

Brent Sackett happened along and found the near dead Julia and took her to a doctor in a nearby settlement; a settlement that was pretty much kept alive by the ruthless rancher and the men who worked for him. The rancher, it seems, hated squatters and had mistaken Julia and the others for just that; squatters!

When Brent arrived at the doctor's office in the small town, two of the men responsible for the killings were also there. Brent wound up killing them in self defense.

When the rancher and a number of his ranch hands rode into the small settlement, Brent had gotten into a shootout with them and wounded the rancher and killed several of his hired hands. Also killed in the gun battle was the town's constable. The others quit fighting when they saw their boss seriously wounded and thought to be dead.

Once Julia was strong enough to travel Brent continued on with her, promising her he would help her get settled in the town of Sundown. He even promised he would help her get the ranch her and her late husband had purchased up and running. Brent was falling in love with the pretty young widow.

Just as Brent and Julia were nearing Sundown, Texas, however, they met up with two men who had just robbed the bank in Sundown. The men's names were Black Jack Haggerty and 'Four Fingers'

Jordan. When Jordan recognized Sackett from Brent's days as a deputy sheriff in Crystal City, a shoot out took place and Brent was severely wounded, but he managed to wound both the bank robbers.

Our story picks up with Julia arriving in the town of Sundown, Texas with a badly wounded Brent Sackett barely hanging on to life. Brent lies in a coma, but is viewing his life in retrospect.

Raymond D. Mason

Chapter

1

JULIA SUMMERS pulled back hard on the reins as she stopped the team of lathered horses in front of the doctor's office in Sundown, Texas. She leaped from the wagon and ran inside the doctor's office.

"Doctor, I have a wounded man outside in the wagon and he's in bad shape. Please help me," Julia said breathlessly.

The doctor hurried outside and looked in the back of the wagon. He could tell by just looking at the wounded man that he was barely hanging on to life.

"Johnny," the doctor yelled to a man on the other side of the street. "Help me get this man inside my office. He's hurt bad."

The young man named Johnny ran across the street and helped carry the near dead Brent Sackett into the doctor's office and the room where he performed his operations.

"Now, Johnny, go and find Jenny Pruitt, I'm going to need her to help me...and hurry, son," the doctor said sternly.

Julia stood by with a worried look on her face and asked, "Is he going to make it, Doctor?"

"Right now, young lady, I really can't say. He's lost a lot of blood and his pulse is very weak. I've got to get the bleeding stopped and then worry about getting the bullets out of him. How'd this happen, anyway," the doctor asked?

"Two men rode up to us as we were on our way into town here, and they just started shooting. Brent...my husband...shot it out with them," Julia explained.

"There were two men robbed the bank here in Sundown just a few hours ago. I'll just bet it was them," the doctor surmised.

"What do you want me to do," Julia asked worriedly?

"Until I get this bleeding stopped, my dear, there's nothing you can do, but stay out of my way and pray. I've got to work fast," the doctor said as pulled the necessary items from his black medical bag.

The doctor started working on Brent and within five minutes, Jenny Pruitt, the woman who acted as his nurse from time to time entered the office. She immediately began helping the doctor; handing him whatever he might need.

The minutes seemed like hours and the hours seemed like days to Julia. The doctor worked feverishly to stop the bleeding. Brent was in such a weakened condition, it was questionable at best, if he would pull through.

The doctor could see that the bullet had to come out, but was in an area that would require a specialist in order to remove it. The operation was much too delicate for him to even attempt to make. Brent was unconscious when Julia had brought him in and nothing had changed.

The doctor looked down at his patient for a moment and then said quietly, "Help me get this bleeding stopped, Lord. I need Your hands guiding me now, and I pray that you have mercy on him."

BRENT SACKETT lay on the operating table unconscious, but his mind was totally alert to something else that he was going through...in his spirit.

He saw himself on a vast desert, tied down hand and foot. He could feel the sun's rays burning through to his very core. His tongue was thick from lack of water and his lips were cracked and swollen.

He was almost blind from staring up into a yellow sky that seemed to crackle and spark from the sun's heat. He tried to speak, but couldn't. He was parched and would give anything for just a drop of water. Brent Sackett felt as though he was in Hell.

Suddenly the yellow sky began to break up and was soon replaced by the most brilliant lights he had ever seen. They were so beautiful; the colors so rich they seemed to be liquid in nature. He saw gold, silver, red, purple, blue, jasper, and green. And the colors seemed to be drawing closer to him.

Along with the colors a cool, gentle breeze began to blow. Brent was transfixed on the colors as they hovered above him. Softly, but with the authority of all Creation a voice spoke to him. The voice was familiar, but he could not put a face with it. Brent knew, however, beyond a shadow of a doubt that the voice belonged to God.

"Brent Sackett, your life hangs in the balance. You must make a decision as to which way you will go," the Voice said to him.

Suddenly Brent saw himself on the edge of a great precipice. It was as if he was watching himself from above as he lay at the edge of the cliff. If he rolled to his left, he would fall into a pitch black hole out of which he would never return. If he rolled to his right, he would roll onto a solid rock; the rock of salvation and eternal life.

Still above his body and looking down he had to make a decision as to which way it would be. As he watched himself balanced on the edge of eternity, he slowly smiled as he watched himself make the decision to live, and rolled on to the rock.

THE DOCTOR glanced down at Brent and saw a smile come to his face. He wondered what was taking place with the young man. It was at precisely that time that the doctor got the bleeding stopped and Brent started to breathe normally. He was still unconscious, but for some reason the doctor felt assured that his patient was going to make it.

Julia didn't really sleep, merely dozed for fifteen to twenty minutes at a time. Every little creak of the wagon or a noise from outside would have her sitting straight up in anticipation of the doctor coming to tell her Brent's condition.

Something else extraordinary happened at that moment also. As the doctor was working over Brent the slug seemed to emerge by itself to a point that the doctor was able to remove it without any trouble, whatsoever! The doctor was shocked. It was as if someone or something was operating on the man from the inside.

A look of questioning amazement spread across the doctor's face. He had never had something like this happen and it caused him to wonder what it was he had just witnessed. Whatever it was, it had just made his job a lot easier and put his patient on the road to full recovery. All he could do then was clean up and wait to see what happened next.

After washing up and cleaning the instruments, the doctor went out in back of his office and climbed up on the wagon. Julia had fallen asleep for one of her short rest periods. Shaking Julia's shoulder very gently the doctor said, "Ma'am, Ma'am...wake up."

Julia opened her eyes and then sat up quickly, "What is it, Doctor...he's going to be all right...oh, please tell me he's going to be all right," she said in a pleading voice.

The doctor smiled, "He's going to be all right. I think he's out of the woods. If nothing changes over the next couple of hours, you can be sure he'll make it. The bleeding has stopped and the bullet has been removed; he's breathing evenly now."

"Oh, thank you, thank you, Doctor. How can I ever thank you enough," Julia said?

"I think you might want to thank God for this. I did all I could and handed your husband over to the Great Physician and He did the rest," the doctor smiled warmly.

"I will, oh yes, I will. When can I see him?"

"You can look in at him right now, but it would be better if you don't try and talk to him, just let him rest; that's what he needs more than anything right now...besides, at the moment he's still under the effects of the sleeping drugs I gave him. Hopefully it won't be long until he is fully conscious again," the doctor said with a smile.

"Maybe I'll be able to get some real sleep myself, now that I know he's going to be all right," Julia said with a faint smile, and then asked. "What about the bullet; were you able to get the slug out of him?"

"I got it...with some help. I had been afraid that it might be too close to the spinal column for me to try and get it out, but something happened that allowed me to remove it with no trouble at all," the doctor said still in wonderment over the experience. He then asked, "Where were you folks headed when this shooting occurred?"

"Right here to Sundown. You see, my husband and I, along with other members of the family and friends were moving here when we were attacked

Ride the Hard Land

by a bunch of men who worked for a rancher who thought we were squatters," Julia said.

"Oh, I see. What happened to the others in your party," the doctor questioned?

"They were all killed by the ones who raided our wagons. It was terrible; simply terrible."

"I understand. Well, your husband should be on his feet again soon. But, even then, he's going to need to be careful for sometime. It will take a lot of care from you. Well, you get some rest and I'll keep an eye on the patient," the doctor said with a smile.

Julia smiled as she nodded her agreement and lay back down on the bed in the wagon. She was asleep and resting for the first time since this ordeal had begun. Her dreams were pleasant for change.

Raymond D. Mason

Chapter 2

JIM CHAUNCEY looked out the saloon doors and called to a man wearing a deputy sheriff's badge.

"Hey, looks like new folks in town. At least new to me," Chauncey said as he watched a covered wagon pulling up in front.

"Oh yeah, we can use some more folks here in Sundown. Is it a family," the deputy named Harmon asked?

"I only see a man on the bench," Chauncey said and then added, "Nope there's a woman just poked her head out from inside the wagon. She ain't bad looking, but nothing to brag about."

"You and your women," Harmon replied with a head shake.

Chauncey continued to look out the window and asked, "Harmon, who owns that wagon that was parked down the street in front of the doctor's office earlier; do you know," Chauncey asked?

"I didn't know there was a wagon parked down there; let me take a look," Harmon stated as he walked over to where Chauncey was standing by the doors and looked towards the doctor's office.

"It's not there now; they moved it around in back late yesterday. I noticed when I rode into town today that it's still back there," Chauncey went on.

"Oh, yeah I did see a wagon parked back there now that you mention it," Harmon replied.

"There was a mighty fine looking little filly that was driving the wagon. Maybe you ought to check it out. You wouldn't want any harm to come to a pretty little thing like her," Chauncey said with a grin.

Just then the man from the wagon that had just pulled up out front walked into the saloon. He went to the bartender and asked how much a bottle of whiskey cost. The bartender told him and the man said he'd take the cheapest bottle they had and added that it was for medicinal purposes. The bartender grinned and set a bottle on the bar.

"Could you tell me where the doctor's office is in town here," the man asked.

"Sure, it's just up the street there; you can't miss it," the bartender answered and then asked, "You got someone ailing, do you?"

"It's our littlest one; he's running a fever and coughing his little head off. I figure a little sip of whiskey will help stop the cough. We'd like the doc to take a look at him though," the man said.

Ride the Hard Land

"He will; he's a good one," the bartender stated.

"Much obliged," the man said as he took his bottle and walked back out to his wagon.

Chauncey and Harmon had continued their conversation and more or less ignored the man buying the whiskey.

"Chauncey, one of these days you're going to push your luck with the ladies you go after and it's going to be aces and eights for you," Harmon said seriously.

"Hey, we all have to go sometime. I'll take my chances. You know what they say Harmon...the milk always tastes sweeter when it's stolen."

"I wouldn't know; I've never stolen milk. I've always paid for whatever I got. Maybe you should do the same," Harmon said.

"Pay for it? Not me...that would be too easy. Don't you like something with a sense of danger to it?"

"My job offers as much danger as I care to indulge in, thank you very much."

"Oh, yeah, like being a deputy here in Sundown is the same as Dodge City, Wichita, or Deadwood when it comes to danger, huh," Chauncey laughed.

"We had a bank robbery just yesterday, remember," Harmon replied?

"Yeah, but look where you are now...sittin' here in the saloon. Why ain't you out with that posse looking for the bank robbers?"

"I wanted to go, but Gray told me he wanted me to stay here in town and make sure nothing happened while he was gone, that's why. He's got plenty of men with him and I'll just bet they catch

19

them men that robbed the bank," Harmon answered back with a little heat in his words.

"Okay, okay, don't get your cinch in a knot. But, seriously, Harmon, I think you ought to check that lady out and see why she's here in Sundown," Chauncey said and then added, "And then report back to me and let me know what she says."

Chauncey continued to look out the window as the man who'd bought the whiskey climbed into his wagon and drove on down the street to the doctor's office.

The man went inside to see if the doctor could take a look at his little boy. After a minute or so the man followed the doctor out and watched as the doctor climbed into the back of the covered wagon. It didn't take him long to see that it was just a case of tonsillitis the boy had.

The man who had sought the doctor was a man by the name of Homer Crandall. The Crandall's were from Abilene, where the Sackett's had their ranch although the two families had never actually met.

Crandall followed the doctor inside and picked up a small bottle of medicine and was told to give the boy one tablespoon full every four hours. Crandall saw Brent lying on the bed in the makeshift operating room and asked about him. The doctor didn't give him any information on his patient.

Chauncey laughed and looked back out the saloon doors. The smile suddenly dropped from his face as he saw a man approaching the saloon on horseback.

"Now, what's he doing in town," Chauncey said under his breath?

"Who's that, Jim," Harmon asked and looked out to see what had caught Chauncey's attention.

Harmon grinned as he recognized the man stepping down off his horse and tying it up at the hitching rail in front of the saloon.

"Abe Hartman, I thought he had gone to Dallas. I guess he's back...and he's packing a gun. I never saw him come into town wearing iron before," Harmon said growing a little more serious.

Chauncey swallowed hard as he watched Hartman tie the bridle reins to the hitching rail and adjust the gun he was wearing on his hip.

"I think I'd better make myself scarce, Harmon. You haven't seen me today, okay," Chauncey said as he hurried towards the back door.

Hartman entered the saloon just as Chauncey was opening the back door.

"Jim Chauncey...you stop where you are," Hartman barked out loudly.

Chauncey froze in his tracks, still facing the back door.

Hartman said firmly, "Turn around and let me look you in the face as I inform the deputy here along with everyone else in this saloon that you are a low down, stinking skunk, and I'm going to shoot you down like I would a rabid dog."

"I don't know what's got your dander up, Abe, but you're wrong about whatever it is that's bothering you," Chauncey said looking over his right shoulder, but not turning around.

"Don't play innocent with me, Chauncey; June told me all about how you came out there while I was gone and tried to force yourself on her," Hartman said with a set jaw.

"Abe, I didn't do anything...I swear on my dead mother's grave I didn't. I rode by there, that's true, but I only stopped and asked if I could water my horse. June invited me in for a cup of coffee and a piece of pie that she said she'd just made.

"I went in and had the pie and coffee and then I left. That's all that happened," Chauncey said pleadingly as he slowly turned to face his accuser.

"She showed me the bruise and scratch marks on her arm where you grabbed her and tried to throw her on the bed. You're a liar along with being a no good lowdown snake, Chauncey. Now, go for your gun," Hartman snapped.

"Bring June in and let her face me when she says I made advances towards her, Abe. I guarantee she'll change her story when I'm present," Chauncey said.

"I promised my brother that I'd look after June when he died. You're the first man to step over the line and I have to honor the promise I made to my brother," Hartman stated.

Chauncey looked at Harmon and pleaded, "You're the law here. You're supposed to stop things like this. He just threatened to kill me and you heard him."

"Hey, until he actually does something my hands are tied," Harmon stated.

Ride the Hard Land

"Enough talk; go for that gun you're wearing," Abe said taking a step towards Chauncey.

The two men stood staring at one another for several seconds. Suddenly Chauncey's hand moved for his gun. Abe Hartman beat Chauncey to the draw by almost a full second, but when he pulled the trigger on his revolver nothing happened.

The hollow sounding click caused Hartman's eyes to widen considerably. Chauncey pulled the trigger on his pistol and the room was filled with the sound of the lone gunshot. Hartman fell to the floor mortally wounded.

Everyone looked on in stunned silence as the smell of spent gunpowder hung in the air. Chauncey looked at Harmon and said quickly, "You saw it, it was a fair fight."

"Yeah, it was a fair fight. You went for your gun first and Abe beat you to the draw. I don't know what happened to his pistol," Harmon said.

"I beat him to the draw! You saw it; he's the one laying on the floor, not me," Chauncey said with a slight grin.

"I'll have to agree that Abe came in looking for a fight. He wouldn't let you back out of the fight and he's dead now. You're innocent of any wrong doing, Chauncey, and I'll tell that to Gray when he gets back," Harmon stated and then added.

"If I was you, though, I'd get out of Sundown as soon as possible. Abe has a lot of friends around here and they're not going to take too kindly to his being gunned down," Harmon said in deadly earnest.

23

Chauncey looked around the room and then hurried towards the door. He hurried out the front doors of the saloon and swung into the saddle of his horse. He headed for the rooming house where his belongings were.

Chapter

3

BRIAN SACKETT rode slowly down the long road to the Sackett ranch house. It was nearing sundown and there were already lamps lit in the big house. He could imagine the family preparing for dinner and the thought caused him to kick his horse into an easy lope.

Just as he was tying his horse up at the hitching rail in front of the house, one of the ranch hands that worked for the Sackett's walked out of the bunk house.

"BJ is that you," the ranch hand called out?

Brian looked around and gave a wave, "Yeah, Stumpy, it's me all right. Man, does this place look good," Brian said and then added, "In fact, even you look good to me."

Raymond D. Mason

"You must have been on the trail a long time, BJ," Stumpy laughed. "The family will sure be glad to see you."

"No more than I will be to see them. You don't know how much I've missed Ma's home cooking. Hey, I'll see you tomorrow, Stumpy. I've gotta put on the feedbag," Brian stated with a big smile.

"It's good to have you home," Stumpy said as he headed in the direction of the out house.

Brian opened the door and walked into the living room expecting someone to be in there. The room was empty, except for him. He walked to the kitchen door and opened it just enough to peer inside.

The only one in the kitchen was Mrs. Sackett and she was heading towards the dining room with a platter of golden fried chicken. The rest of the family was seated around the large table and waiting for Mrs. Sackett to join them with the final dish.

Brian watched her and let her get into the dining room before walking in behind her.

"Mm, mm; how'd you know I was coming home tonight," Brian said as he pushed the door open and entered the dining room.

"Brian, thank God you're home," Mrs. Sackett said as she set the platter down and wiped her hands on her apron before rushing over and throwing her arms around Brian's neck.

"Hey, welcome back, kid, "AJ said as he stood up along with John Sackett.

"Tell us all about your journey. My lord it's been a long time since you lit out of here," John went on.

Brian started answering questions as he sat down and started filling a plate with fried chicken, mashed potatoes, gravy, green beans, corn on the cob, and a hot cup of coffee.

He talked between mouthfuls and told them the high points of his journey. The one point he hesitated in telling them, however, was that he'd seen Brent. He didn't know how he would handle their questions.

When he felt the time was right to tell them he wouldn't tell them that Brent was on the run from the law. He'd wait until he felt they were ready to handle hearing that bit of news. For now, however, he'd leave off the bad news.

The questions and answers went on until Brian couldn't keep his eyes open anymore. Finally he laughed and said, "I'm going to have to get some shuteye, or you may be digging a grave for me in the morning."

They all laughed and said goodnight. Brian went up to his room and was asleep within seconds after his head hit the feather pillow on his bed. He was in for the best night's sleep he'd had since he'd left the ranch.

BRIAN AWOKE rested and ready to go to work. He had been gone from the Sackett ranch for over six months and if felt good to be back home and doing what he'd been meant to do; ranching.

The aroma of fresh made coffee mingled with that of hot biscuits had drifted from the kitchen to his bedroom. He quickly dressed and hurried downstairs. His mother and sister were busy preparing breakfast and Brian was the first of the Sackett men to come down.

"I thought that smell would bring you running," his sister laughed when she saw Brian.

"You don't know how much I've missed Ma and your, cooking. I haven't had a decent meal since I left here. Nobody out there can cook like you two. You could make a fortune if you ever decide to open a café," Brian grinned.

"What; and have to feed forty or fifty like you three times a day; no thank you," Brian's mother said with a laugh.

"Yeah, I guess you both have it kind of soft here, huh," Brian teased.

"Just for that you can't have any breakfast," his sister came back.

"I surrender; you win," Brian said just as the kitchen door opened and John Sackett, Brian's father walked in.

"What's this about surrendering? Who are you surrendering to," John asked?

"Brian surrendered to us so he could have breakfast," his sister answered.

"Oh, well I don't blame him one bit for that. How long before we eat," John asked?

"By the time you get washed up it will be on the table. Where's AJ," Mrs. Sackett asked?

"He's on his way down," John replied.

Brian and John went to the kitchen pump and washed their face and hands. Before they had finished AJ had joined them. They went to the large table in the dining room and took their usual seats.

They said grace and began to have their breakfast, noticing that Brian had something on his mind. Finally John asked his son what was troubling him.

"Well, I have good news and I wanted to wait until the new had worn off my return to give it to you. Brent is alive," Brian said, getting some stunned looks from the family members.

"Brent's alive...," his mother said.

"Yeah, but he's still bitter about the War. He said he'd have to have time to heal before coming back here," Brian said, stretching the truth considerably.

"Did you tell him he's always welcome here," John asked?

"Yeah, I told him; but, he said he had to work it out in his own mind. He sent his love to everyone and said to tell you he misses you," Brian went on.

"Where is he living," his mother wanted to know?

"He's just drifting around right now. He doesn't stay in one place very long," Brian went on. "We only talked for about an hour and then he said goodbye. I just wanted to let you know that he's not dead and could show up here some day. Hopefully it will be sooner than later."

The family took over the conversation and began recalling some of the funny things that had happened when all the boys were living at home. Soon AJ changed the subject to the day's chores.

"Are you up to going up around Griffin Flat with me today and checking on something I spotted the other day when I was up there," AJ asked Brian?

"Sure I am. What is it you want to do?"

"I just want your opinion on something. I'll tell you on the way up there," AJ said with a slight frown that signaled to Brian he didn't want to talk about it right then.

"Okay. I'll fill you in on a few things I found out on my journey," Brian replied, meaning what he'd learned about Brent.

"Pa, we might not make it back by sundown, so don't worry about us. We'll take enough supplies with us. I want to show Brian several things while we're up at Griffin Flat," AJ stated, getting an agreeing nod from his pa.

John nodded his approval and then said, "You might even check on Shorty while you're up there. I know it would be out of your way, but I'd hate to think he's run out of something at the line shack."

"Yeah, okay...we'll do that," AJ agreed.

Ride the Hard Land

Chapter 4

AFTER a big breakfast Brian and AJ saddled up and headed for Griffin Flat. Brian didn't press AJ about what it was he'd said he wanted to discuss with him, but he knew something was on AJ's mind. Finally AJ looked over at Brian and spoke up.

"This morning at breakfast, I told you I wanted to discuss something with you...remember," he started?

"Yeah, I remember...so what's her name? Do I know her," Brian asked with a knowing grin?

"Now what makes you think it's a woman," AJ said quickly?

"Well, isn't it," Brian laughed?

"You know me too well, little brother. That is one of the things I wanted to talk to you about," AJ replied.

"Oh, and what's the other thing?"

Ride the Hard Land

"Indians...Comanche I think. I'll show you the sign I saw up near Griffin Flat. We've heard rumors that there is a war party in the area. You'll see when we get there."

"Okay, let's talk about the most important subject to you," Brian said holding back a grin.

"Well, you know it's going to be about Millie," AJ said quickly.

"Millie...you mean Millie Patterson? Don't tell me you've fallen for Millie. You're going to be the most hated man in Texas if she marries you. Every guy who has ever laid eyes on her wants to marry her; didn't you know that," Brian said and gave a long whistle. "Millie Patterson."

"We've been seeing each other for about four months. She said she loves me, and I love her. I'm going to ask her to marry me when we get back off this little trip. So what do you think; do you think she will say yes," AJ pressed?

"I don't know; she might. You do know that Ward Potter asked her, don't you?"

"She said she never really was in love with him."

"You could have fooled folks that saw the two of them together. She stuck to him like a sick cat to a hot rock," Brian said. "And what about Billy Watson; he thought they were all but ready to walk down the aisle and then saw her with Steve Dubbins," Brian added.

"Do you really think she's that fickle?"

"I don't know...maybe they were just more anxious to get married than she was; hey, we're talking about a woman here. It's like trying to figure out a wild mustang, for crying out loud. Who knows what goes on inside their head," Brian stated with a chuckle.

"Yeah, not like us men, huh? They know what goes on inside our head...usually nothing," AJ said and they both broke out in laughter.

Brian looked at his brother and could see he was desperately seeking some brotherly advice. He thought for a moment and then gave what he considered to be good advice.

"AJ, all you can do is to ask Millie if she'll be your wife. If she says yes, you're in; if she says no, you join the list of suitors she's rejected. The choice is yours...at this point."

"Okay, I'll take my chances and see what she says. You're right, little brother, I have to rely on what she wants," AJ said nodding his head.

Brian thought about what he wanted to say to AJ about Brent. He knew he could be more open with AJ than with the rest of the family. He figured the best approach was head on.

"AJ, Brent couldn't come home even if he wanted to," Brian started his conversation about Brent.

"Why is that? What's he been up to," AJ wanted to know.

"Brent has changed a lot since the War," Brian said and then paused. "He's a man on the dodge."

"You're not serious? Brent...an outlaw; why, what did he do?"

"He killed a couple of lawmen for one thing. You know what that means. Every sheriff and marshal will shoot first and ask questions later where Brent's concerned," Brian answered.

"Yeah, they tend to do that, all right. How'd you learn about it?"

"Well, he told me when I met him down in San Antone. And then several lawmen mistook me for him once a photograph of him hit the wanted posters. He'd worked as a deputy in Crystal City, but killed the sheriff there and took it on the run. There was some stolen money involved from what I heard," Brian stated.

"At least we know he didn't die on a battlefield somewhere. I wish he'd come back here, though; maybe we could help him get out of the mess he's in," AJ said thoughtfully.

"He did do one good thing. He's going under a different name. He said he didn't want to bring any shame to the Sackett name. He goes by Dan Johnson now, or at least that's what it was at the time. He'll probably have to change it again though," Brian said.

"I can see why you didn't bring it up to the others. That's going to break Ma and Pa's heart; not to mention Sis," AJ said.

"I figured I'd just keep that information to myself; but, I thought you should know," Brian said.

"I'm glad you did, Brian; I truly am."

The two grew silent as they both drifted off into their own thoughts. They picked up their pace slightly, giving their mounts a little more free rein.

WHEN THEY arrived at the spot where AJ had seen the signs of what appeared to be a Comanche war party, they reined up. They found plenty of moccasin tracks on the ground and a large campfire. By the size of the fire and the horse's tracks they figured the raiding party must have been at least fifteen to twenty braves.

"Look over here," AJ said as he walked away from where the large campfire had been.

Brian walked over where his brother was standing and looked at the ground. There were a number of unshod horse tracks, but also several tracks of horses that had been shod, indicating the Comanche's could possibly be riding horses they'd stolen or they could be riding with several Comancheros.

The two brothers looked at one another with stern looks on their face. Brian knelt down and touched the tracks, first the unshod and then the shod ones.

"These tracks aren't that old," AJ said. "No more than four or five days, I'd say. It looks like all the tracks were made around the same time."

"Comanche are bad enough, but throw in Comancheros and you've really got trouble," AJ said.

"Yeah, you've got that right. I wonder which way these jaspers were heading," Brian wondered aloud as he continued to check the tracks.

"I figure the Indians were joined by the Comancheros here at this campsite. The Comanche came in from due north and the Comancheros from the north/west. When they left they all headed southeast. I'll show you," AJ said motioning for Brian to follow him.

They walked a good piece out of the camp to the north and AJ showed his brother the tracks leading in from both directions. Brian agreed with AJ's assessment of the rendezvous.

Brian followed AJ to another spot that would indicate the Indians along with the Comancheros had headed southeast when they left the campsite. Fortunately the Sackett ranch house was southwest.

Brian thought for a moment and then said, "Do we have anyone staying in the line shack by Possum Creek; because that's the direction they're headed?"

AJ looked serious as he replied, "Yeah, Abner Sikes."

"Maybe we'd better check on him. How long has he been down there?"

"About two weeks. We can go and check on him first and then swing back around and check on Shorty at the other line shack," AJ said.

"We may as well; I think we can make it to Possum Creek by sundown," Brian said.

"Easy. We'll have to spend the night, though. If Abner's running low on something we'll have to bring it back later. The same holds for Shorty," AJ said thoughtfully.

"What are we waiting for, let's ride," Brian said as he turned and headed for his horse with AJ following.

Raymond D. Mason

Chapter

5

BILL NUGENT pulled the wagon to a halt and told his wife to listen. The two of them sat very still, even holding their breath slightly in order to hear a little better. Bill suddenly looked at his wife, Tanya and stated, "That's gunfire; it's far off, but it's gunfire for sure."

"Do you think we ought to go and see what it's about," Tanya asked in a concerned voice?

"I would, but I don't want to risk it with you along," Bill said shaking his head no.

"But what if it's a family in need of help, Bill? I think we should go."

"And what if it's a band of Comanche; we might be riding to our death. I won't put you in danger like that," Bill said firmly. "If we should run into a marshal or a cavalry patrol; or, possibly a Texas

Ranger we'll tell them what we heard," he said with the gunfire still audible in the distance.

"I just hate to think there might be women and children involved," Tanya insisted.

"I hate the thought, too, but the answer is still the same. No, we're not going," Bill said with finality.

With that he turned the team of horses to the northwest and moved off away from the sound of the distant gunfire. He did, however, cast a continual glance in the direction of the noise just in case someone was being chased their way.

They had traveled about a half mile before Nugent pulled the team to a halt once more so he could listen again. The gunshots were louder than they had been earlier. Whoever was doing the shooting was on the move, and it sounded as if they were heading in their direction.

Nugent began looking for a place they might be able to make a stand if it was Indians. Looking off to their right he saw where they might be able to take cover if need be; a small arroyo with trees for cover.

Nugent reined the horses towards the arroyo and then down the slight embankment near the grove of trees. Here they would be able to observe without being seen; that is unless whoever was headed their way decided to head for the arroyo and the cover of the trees as well. If it was Comanche then they'd be riding into rifle fire.

Four riders topped the rise, whipping their mounts with their bridle reins to keep them at full gallop. Not more than two hundred yards behind them were sixteen Comanche warriors and four Comancheros.

When the four riders saw the arroyo and trees they headed straight towards them. Bill Nugent frowned and gritted his teeth as the men aimed their mounts in their direction.

"Danged idiots, they'll lead that bunch right to us. Nothing left to do now, but help them shoot it out," Nugent said more to himself than to his wife.

The four riders saw the wagon and reined their horses in its direction. At least there would be one more gun to help them fend off the war party. When they reached the wagon they pulled their rifles from their scabbards and dismounted, hitting the ground running.

"Man, are you a welcome sight," one of the men said.

"I wish I could say the same," Nugent replied, causing the man to give him a questioning look.

The men took up their positions and aimed at the oncoming band of renegades. The taller of the men barked out an order that indicated he was the leader of the other three.

"Take careful aim. Gene, you work from the far left; Sandy, you start from the far right. Bill, you and I will start in the middle and work out; you to the right, and me to the left," the man barked.

"What about me," Nugent asked?

"You shoot any one of them you want to," the man said.

"Okay, Captain, well wait for your first shot," the ranger named Bill said.

41

Nugent looked at the man and that was when he noticed the badge of a Texas Ranger.

"I take it you are all four rangers, am I right," Nugent asked?

"Right," the man they called 'Captain' answered and then added, "We'll take care of introductions after we dispose of this bunch. Wait for my command to fire."

The marauding Indians and Comancheros drew closer. Nugent kept wondering when the 'Captain' was going to give the command to open fire. Finally it came.

"Now, fire," the Captain shouted.

The five of them opened up on their targets and fired in rapid succession. Bullets kicked up dust around them as well. Being able to take aim without being jostled by a galloping horse, the rangers, along with Nugent, picked off Comanche and Comancheros until the number was down to thirteen. Only then did the renegades retreat.

The Captain stood up and stated, "We won't see them again, but somebody will. I hope no homesteaders are in the area."

The Captain then looked at Nugent and said, "That was some good shooting you did there. You've handled a rifle before I figure."

"I was a sniper in the War," Nugent replied seriously.

"I won't ask what side you were on," the captain said with a wry smile. He then asked, "Where are you folks headed?"

Ride the Hard Land

"We're on our way to Abilene. We're going in to pick up some much needed supplies. Where are you rangers headed," Nugent asked?

"Actually we're headed up to a small town near Lubbock; called Sundown. We've got word that there was a bank robbery up there and they're in need of some rangers," the Captain replied.

"Isn't it unusual for four rangers to go out on a bank robbery," Nugent asked curiously?

"Not when the gang is thought to be the Black Jack Haggerty gang," the captain stated.

"Oh, that explains it. By the way, my name is Bill Nugent and this is my wife Tanya," Nugent said.

"It's nice to make your acquaintance, folks. I'm Captain Culpepper and this is Bill McNiece, Sandy Knapp, and Gene House."

"I guess I owe you an apology for the way I behaved when I saw you men heading down into this arroyo. I was hoping you'd go on by, and lead the Comanche war party away from us," Nugent said truthfully.

The Captain chuckled, "It's a good thing we joined you. If they'd spotted your wagon tracks you'd both be without your hair about now."

"Yeah, I guess you're right. Well, we shouldn't have anymore trouble with that bunch," Nugent said and moved back to the wagon.

"We'll ride along with you to Abilene," the Captain stated.

43

Raymond D. Mason

Chapter 6

JIM CHAUNCEY rode into Lubbock, Texas and stopped at the first saloon he came to. He stepped down off his horse and took a long look up and down the main street. He grinned as he noticed the number of women on the boardwalk doing their shopping.

"Thank you Abe Hartman. This looks good to me," Chauncey said with a leering eye. "Yes siree, this looks mighty good to me."

Chauncey looped his bridle reins around the hitching rail and tied them before walking up the steps to the saloon entrance. He pushed the doors open and looked around the room.

Since it was Saturday, there were already a number of cowhands in the saloon and the place was about two thirds full. Chauncey walked over to the bar and caught the bartender's attention.

"If you were a gambler which poker game would you want to sit in on," he asked and looked at the four tables that had games going on?

"The game with the man in the bowler hat; but be careful, he can be mean when riled," the bartender stated.

"Thanks, I'll see to it that you get a little something when I win," Chauncey said.

"I can use it," the bartender grinned.

Chauncey walked over to the table and waited for someone to look in his direction. The man in the bowler hat was the first to do so.

"Howdy, mind if I sit in," Chauncey asked?

"If you've got the money to do so, welcome," the man in the bowler answered.

"I do," Chauncey said and sat down in the empty seat.

He pulled two hundred dollars out of his pocket and set it in front of him. The banker asked him how he wanted the money in chips and Chauncey gave his order. He set the four stacks of chips in front of him and looked around the table.

"Let's play poker, gentlemen," Chauncey said with a slight grin.

The men all looked at the newcomer and nodded their approval. The man in the bowler dealt out the hand. Chauncey could tell the man was experienced with a deck of card and had to be a professional. He guessed that the bartender had a deal going with the man in the bowler.

Chauncey lost the first two hands, but won the third one. He took in over one hundred dollars and had pegged the bowler hat man exactly right. This man could handle a deck of cards. This was not going to be easy, but Chauncey felt he was up to the task.

Finally Chauncey made an announcement to those at the table.

"Gentlemen, I have a business meeting here in town at the Wells Fargo Bank, so this will be my last hand until the meeting is over. I just wanted you to know that. I do plan on coming back once I've completed my business. I hope you will all still be here," he said.

He had waited until the deal came around to him before declaring it to be his last hand. He wanted to walk away a winner and if things went the way they should, he would do just that.

The man in the bowler watched him closely. Chauncey shuffled the cards skillfully. As he dealt the cards out the light reflected off one of them in such a way he knew what the card was even though it was face down. The deck was marked and someone at the table was the beneficiary of it.

Chauncey looked quickly at the players' faces and quickly spotted the cheater. It was a man wearing glasses and a bowler hat. The glasses were shaded just enough to allow the wearer to identify each card dealt.

Chauncey's scheme would be much harder to pull off now; what with one of the men knowing what each player held in his hand. The thing was how could the card cheater expose him without tipping his own cheating as well? He couldn't.

"I don't think I've ever seen glasses like yours before, friend," Chauncey said looking straight at the man in the bowler. "Where'd you get them?"

"I had them made the last time I went to St. Louis...why do you ask?"

"I'd like to have a pair just like them. I'll bet the shaded lens really helps your eyesight, huh," Chauncey said getting a questioning look from the men at the table.

"Could I try them on to see if I'd like them," Chauncey asked?

"No, I don't let people try my glasses on. It stretches them," the man said.

"I won't put them on, then. I just want to see how much it helps your eyesight, that's all," Chauncey pressed.

"Look, play cards; I'm not here to try and sell shaded glasses for the guy who made these," the cheater snapped back angrily.

"Is there something else about those glasses that you don't want the rest of us to know," Chauncey went on?

"No...let's play cards and knock off the palaver, okay," the bowler man said.

Chauncey pulled his Derringer out of his vest pocket and held it under the table, aimed at the man's midsection. He wasn't about to make an allegation against the man without having a definite edge.

"Take the glasses off and hand them to the man to your left...or get ready to die," Chauncey said bravely since he had the drop on the man.

He went on, "I want you to put the glasses on and take a look at the back of the cards on the table. Tell me and the others here, what you see," Chauncey said evenly.

The man did as he was told and after a couple of seconds said, "Well, I'll be; you can read what the cards are when you look through these glasses."

"You no good cheat," one of the men at the table snapped.

"Go get the sheriff; there's no need to go crazy here," Chauncey said loudly.

The man in the derby sat with both his hands atop the poker table, but his eyes darted around the room at the angry faces. He knew what happened to card cheats and he wasn't about to let that happen to him.

Suddenly he jumped to his feet, turning the table over in the process and sending cards, money, whiskey and beer glasses flying towards Chauncey. A natural reflex caused Chauncey to pull the trigger of the Derringer as he fell backwards; the bullet hit the cheater in the head.

The man grabbed for his face as he fell backwards. The bullet had hit him in the forehead. The crowd stood looking at him in stunned silence. Then they looked at Chauncey. He looked stunned as well.

Someone said excitedly, "You just killed Boston Bailey."

Chauncey looked around at the man who'd made the statement and asked, "Who's he?"

"He's the fastest gun around these parts, I'll tell you that," the man stated.

Raymond D. Mason

"That's Boston Bailey," someone else added?

"You'll be famous around here, Mister," another said.

"Every fast gun in the territory will be looking to make a name for him self by killing the man who beat Boston Bailey," another said.

"I'm not a gunfighter. He was cheating. I already had my gun drawn," Chauncey said trying to deflect what might become a reputation for being fast with a gun.

"Boston's sidekick will be the first to come looking for you. Some say he's faster than Boston Bailey; the two never got around to proving either way, though," the bartender said.

Just then the sheriff walked up to the overturned table and looked down at Bailey. He looked around at the gathering and then asked, "Who did this?"

"He did," several people responded, pointing at Chauncey.

"Did he go for his gun," the sheriff asked?

"Yeah, I caught him cheating and called him on it, Sheriff. I wanted to turn him over to you, but he jumped up and went for his gun," Chauncey stated.

"That's right, Sheriff," one of the card players stated. "He said we should send for you when Bailey went for his gun."

"You beat Boston Bailey. You'll be a famous man around here, Mister. What's your name," the sheriff asked?

"Chauncey, but I'm not a gunfighter. I had the drop on him and the gun went off when he jumped up.

"Don't matter none, Chauncey. You took him down. If I was you I'd get out of town before word gets out. We have a couple of fast gun hands right here in Lubbock that will be looking to try you," the sheriff said advisedly.

"I'll be moving on, Sheriff. I'm no gunman," Chauncey stated.

"Go ahead. I can see you acted in self defense," the sheriff said looking down at Bailey.

Chauncey picked up his money and hurried out of the saloon. He mounted up and headed out of town at a fast gallop. He'd want to put as much distance as he could between himself and Lubbock. He figured he could visit his sister in Abilene. He wouldn't be that well known there; or so he hoped.

Chauncey had killed two men within twelve hours. Both men were quite capable with a gun and one had even built up a reputation. Chauncey's life was in the process of taking a huge change in direction.

Raymond D. Mason

Chapter 7

JULIA SUMMERS looked down at Brent Sackett and smiled tenderly. Brent had regained consciousness and it looked like he was going to make a full recovery from his gunshot wound.

"How long was I out," Brent asked?

"About a day and a half, but the doctor says you're going to be back to normal before too long," Julia said softly.

"I'm glad to see that you weren't hurt during the shootout...you weren't, were you," Brent asked concernedly?

"No, no I wasn't hurt. I was worried sick, though. I was so afraid I wouldn't get you to a doctor before you...in time for him to help you, I mean," Julia said as she looked deep into Brent's eyes.

"Something happened while I was unconscious; something very real, but very strange. I'll tell you about it someday, but now's not the time," Brent said thoughtfully.

Julia nodded her head slowly. She leaned forward and kissed Brent tenderly on the lips. As she pulled away she smiled and said, "The doctor lined me up with a couple of local men who are going to help us get settled in the house my husband bought.

"I told them I'll go out with them tomorrow and start getting the place ready for us to move in," Julia informed Brent.

"Give me a few days and I can do it," Brent said seriously.

"No you don't. The doctor said he doesn't want you doing anything for at least three weeks to a month. He said he wants you near his office for at least another two, maybe three days," Julia replied.

"By that time I'll have the house set up and ready for you. I'll get you back on your feet," Julia said with a smile.

"Julia...," Brent started to say and then paused, "I'm not going to be able to stay after I'm well enough to ride."

Brent paused before continuing, "There's something I have to tell you. I know this could change our relationship when I tell you, but I have to get this off my chest."

Julia looked at Brent with questioning in her eyes as he paused for a moment and then went on.

"Julia, I'm a man with a price on his head. I've got the law after me for some things I've done and I don't want you to be involved. You're in danger every moment you're with me," Brent said evenly.

"I don't care, Brent. If you did something wrong you must have had a good reason. I can't believe you're a man who would intentionally do bad things. You'll feel different when you get on your feet again. Where our place is located, no one is going to come poking around there. The ones looking for you may never know you're in this area," Julia said shaking her head negatively.

"They all ready know I'm in the area. At least they know a stranger with a bullet wound is in town," Brent argued.

"The bank had just been robbed here in Sundown and the men who shot you must be the ones who robbed it.

"When we got here I explained to the doctor that two men had tried to rob us. He said the sheriff was out with a posse looking for the men. He asked me your name and I told him Dan Burton. You don't have to worry about anyone recognizing you now, I'm sure," Julia said with a pleading look on her pretty face.

"See what I mean. You don't even know my full name. My full name is Brent Sackett."

"I don't care what it is. You could be Jesse James and it wouldn't change the way I fell about you," Julia said with tears in her eyes.

"Okay, okay...Let's drop it for a few days. We'll talk about it later, okay," Brent said feeling a little tired.

"Okay, Brent; get some rest. I have to go pick up a few things from the store. I love you...no matter what name you are," Julia said.

"Julia, before you leave would you do one favor for me," Brent asked politely?

"If I can, you know I will," Julia replied.

"Just so I feel more secure, would you give me my pistol. I think I'll rest a little easier if I have it within easy reach," Brent said.

Julia thought about it for a moment and then smiled as she nodded her head yes, "Yes, I'll get your gun for you."

She went to the wagon where she had left it and took the gun out of the holster and carried it back to the doctor's office. When she handed it to Brent she noticed how he physically relaxed. He put the gun under his pillow so it would be within easy reach.

Chapter 8

BRIAN AND AJ topped a hill that gave them a good view of the line shack at Possum Creek where their ranch hand, Abner Sikes was staying. They reined up and scoured the area in the valley below looking for any sign that might tell them Abner was there.

AJ looked down at the ground and then cast a quick glance at Brian. Brian noticed and asked, "What is it?"

"Look down...those unshod pony tracks look fresh and they lead straight down this hill towards the line shack. I'm afraid Abner might have had guests for dinner last night," AJ said, causing Brian to look at the Indian pony tracks.

"They usually burn the buildings though. Why is the line shack still standing," Brian said thoughtfully.

"Maybe they have plans for it. I think we'd better go in from different directions. There might be someone inside the shack besides Abner," AJ suggested, getting an agreeing nod from Brian.

The two split up with Brian heading off to the right of AJ so he would be coming in from the side of the shack while AJ came in from the front. They both pulled their Winchesters from their scabbards and held them ready for action.

They reached the line shack at the same time. AJ stopped his horse about twenty yards from the front of the line shack and took another quick look around. That gave Brian a chance to get up to the shack from the side without bein seen; there were two windows in the shack; one in the front and one at the back.

Brian crept up to the back window and peeked inside. He couldn't see anyone, but wasn't able to see what was in one corner of the room. He moved around to the front of the shack and motioned for AJ to ride on up. Brian carefully went to the front window and peeked inside, this time able to see the corner he hadn't been able to see from in back.

Brian hurried to the door and opened it quickly. Rushing inside he went straight to the body of the man lying in the corner. It was Abner Sikes. He'd been shot at close range. He was dead.

AJ entered the shack as Brian stood up and gave him the bad news.

"He's dead, AJ. Whoever did it was standing very close to him. I don't think the Indians did it. The question now is why they didn't burn the place," Brian wondered?

Ride the Hard Land

"Was his horse in back," AJ asked?

"Yeah, it was. That's funny too. Comanche's usually take the horses with them. There again, why didn't they this time," Brian questioned?

"Maybe what we've been reading as Indian ponies isn't that at all. Maybe it's whites riding unshod horses. There has to be a reason for the change of tactics by this bunch," AJ surmised.

"We'll take Abner's body back to the ranch for burial. We might as well get started," Brian said.

"Yeah; grab his saddle there and we'll load him up," AJ said as he picked up the saddle blanket and bridle off the floor.

Brian went out back and took the hobbles off Abner's horse and saddled it up. They had just started loading the dead man's body on the horse when a cavalry patrol appeared over a hill top.

AJ looked up as the detail started down the slope towards them and said, "There's the reason for the change of tactics by the Comanche renegades."

The cavalry patrol rode up to where they were and stopped. The lieutenant in charge gave them a curious look before speaking.

"Looks like there was some trouble here," the lieutenant stated.

"There was. It looks like a band of Comanche renegades went through here a couple of days ago. We followed unshod pony tracks that led straight to the line shack," AJ stated while Brian continued securing Abner's body to his horse.

"Did you know this man," the lieutenant asked?

59

"He worked for us. My name is AJ Sackett and this is my brother Brian," AJ provided.

"I see," the lieutenant said thoughtfully and then asked, "You're not related to a Brent Sackett, by any chance, are you?"

The two brothers cast a quick glance to one another before Brian answered, "He's my twin brother. Why do you ask that?"

"We've had some telegrams from various lawmen that should we run across him to arrest him for murder. Did you know he was a man on the run?"

Brian slowly nodded his head yes, "Yeah, I knew it. He isn't around here, though; I can tell you that."

"Do you know where he's at," the lieutenant asked?

"The last time I saw him was in San Antone and that was a couple of months back," Brian said honestly.

"We received word not too long ago that a man answering his description shot it out with a constable and a rancher and his men. He rode away without a scratch, but left a number of dead and wounded men in his wake," the lieutenant stated.

"But you don't know that it was Brent, right," AJ asked?

"No, just that the man answered your brother's description."

"Like I said, he was in San Antonio the last time I saw him," Brian restated.

"Where are you taking the dead man's body, if you don't mind my asking," the cavalry officer asked?

"Back to our ranch in Abilene; he'll be buried in our cemetery back there," AJ replied.

"Well, we won't hold you men any longer. You've got a considerable ride ahead of you."

"By the way, Lieutenant; were you bivouacked around here," AJ questioned.

"Yes, last night we made camp just beyond that hill there. Why do you ask?"

"Just wondering; that could be why the Comanche renegades didn't burn the line shack. They didn't want you to see the glow from the fire or the smoke," AJ stated.

"Where'd you see those tracks, Sackett," the lieutenant asked, looking at AJ.

"Right over there," AJ said pointing in the direction they had seen the tracks, "Coming down the hillside there."

"Thanks, we'll pick 'em up. You men have a safe trip back to your ranch," the lieutenant said and motioned for his troopers to follow him.

AJ and Brian watched them ride in the direction of the Comanche's tracks for a moment before finishing up with the securing of Abner's body to the saddle.

AJ turned and looked at Brian and said thoughtfully, "Let's go back to the ranch by way of Uncle Carl's place. I want to talk to him about buying a horse he had the last time I was there."

"Okay, but it's a good half days ride out of the way. Abner is going to start getting a little ripe, don't you think," Brian said with a frown.

"I guess you're right. The horse can wait. First things first," AJ said with a half grin.

AJ suddenly had a thought. He looked off in the distance and then turned and looked in the opposite direction before speaking.

Brian noticed his brother's actions and commented, "What is it? What are you thinking about?"

"If we go over that hill over there," AJ said, pointing to a hill about three miles away, "we could catch the stagecoach road and head home by it."

"That's right; it would sure make the traveling easier. What are we waiting for," Brian said as he stepped up on his horse.

The two of them headed for the stagecoach road with Brian leading Abner's horse and AJ leading their pack animal.

THE BAND of Comanche renegades and the Comancheros who had joined up with them, sat astride their horses among the rocks that overlooked the stagecoach road below. They could see a good two miles in either direction from their vantage point and were waiting for the stagecoach scheduled to pass there at any moment.

The leader of the Comancheros was a man by the name of Pacer Reyes, a half breed and a man wanted by the law in three states. The leader of the Comanche's was a young man by the name of Iron Eyes.

Reyes pulled his pocket watch out of his vest pocket and checked the time. He then stood up in the stirrups and looked to the north before saying to Iron Eyes, "That coach should be along here anytime now."

"And you say coach has much money on it? Money to buy many rifles and food and blankets," Iron Eyes said with a frown.

"Yes, much money for those things. Your share will buy you one hundred rifles and much food and blankets," Reyes assured him.

Iron Eyes thought for a moment and then asked, "What do you do with your share of money?"

"Buy more rifles for us; more ammunition to kill white eyes," Reyes said knowing how the mind of Iron Eyes worked.

Reyes didn't trust the Comanche's at all. He knew they would take what they wanted if push came to shove. He had to make it appear that the Comancheros' share of the money would be used in the same way the Comanche's share would be used.

One of the Comancheros called to Reyes, "Here it comes, Pacer."

Reyes and Iron Eyes looked in the direction the man was pointing and could see the stagecoach about a mile away. Iron Eyes motioned for his braves to follow him and he reined his horse down the hillside between the rocks towards a stand of trees alongside the road.

Reyes and his men rode down the hill behind the Comanche war party but stopped among some rocks on the opposite side of the road from the trees. This was a perfect spot for a holdup.

The coach rumbled down the road with the driver and the man riding shotgun ready for anything. They had heard rumors of Comancheros and the renegade war party being in that part of the country.

The guard leaned over and yelled to the men inside the coach, "Be ready, we're nearing a good spot for a holdup."

The two male passengers pulled their pistols just in case there was a robbery attempt. As the coach neared the spot where the Indians and Comancheros were waiting, one of the coach's horses started to limp. The driver noticed and pulled the coach to a halt.

"What is it Ed," the man riding shotgun asked?

"One of my lead horses is limping," I'll have to check and see if he picked up a rock in his horseshoe," Ed said as he started to climb down.

The coach had stopped slightly out of range of the rifles of those lying in wait. All the desperados could do then was to wait until the driver checked his horse's hoof and moved on towards them. The one thing they didn't want to do was lose the element of surprise.

Chapter

9

BRIAN AND AJ reined up atop a ridge that gave them a good view of the stagecoach road below where the stagecoach had stopped.

"Looks like the stage has a problem with one of their horses," Brian said when he noticed the coach's driver tending to the horse's hoof.

AJ was looking further ahead of the coach at something that had caught his attention. He focused on the object for several moments and then said excitedly.

"It looks like that coach stopped just in time, Brian...look up ahead of it. Is that what I think it is in the trees down there," AJ said.

Brian looked in the direction of AJ's gaze and came to the same conclusion.

"You've got that right, big brother. I make about a dozen in those trees," Brian stated.

"Let's get down there before that driver finishes attending to his horse," AJ said as both men kicked up their mounts and galloped down the hill.

The driver found what the problem was with his lead horse's hoof; he'd been right, it was a rock wedged inside the horseshoe. He pulled his pocket knife out and began trying to dislodge the rock.

He had just got the rock out and put the horse's hoof back on the ground when he heard the sound of approaching horses. He turned and looked in the direction of the two riders who were now within shouting range.

"Stay where you're at," AJ shouted.

The driver called back, "What's that?"

"Stay where you are. Ambush up ahead," AJ yelled again.

"What did he say, Earl," the driver asked his guard?

The guard was standing up and looking in the direction of the stand of trees as he yelled, "We've got company up ahead, Ed."

The Comanche war party saw what was happening and knew they would have to attack the coach. Iron Eyes yelled to his men to mount up. They swung onto their horses and headed out of the trees in the direction of the coach.

"Here they come," Brian said when he saw the Indians come out onto the road.

Brian and AJ tied their horses to the back of the stagecoach and AJ climbed inside. Brian climbed up top with the guard and driver. The guard got down in the boot well of the coach and began firing once the Indians were within range.

Brian lay atop the coach with his rifle and was able to take careful aim at the approaching renegades. Each shot he fired found its mark. AJ had grabbed his Winchester and began firing; the other two men waited until the Comanche's were within range of their pistols.

The Comancheros remained in the rocks to see what happened with the Comanche war party. Reyes figured to let them suffer the heavier casualties. He would wait until they had things more under control before having his men get involved.

Due to the added firepower by the addition of the Sackett's, the war party took on heavy casualties. It was only when Brian knocked Iron Eyes of his horse with a bullet to the leader's shoulder that the other warriors turned back. The war party was only half the size it had been when they attacked.

The driver and guard stood up as the remaining members of the war party retreated. The guard looked at Brian and gave a war whoop.

"Man, am I glad you two boys came along when you did. We owe you a debt of gratitude, young fella, the guard said with a wide grin.

"You can say that again. I'll tell the stage line about you and the other fella's hand in turning back this attack. They may want to show their appreciation in some way," the driver said, slapping Brian on the back.

"It was our pleasure to get involved in this little fracas. This bunch killed one of our wranglers; that's his body on that horse back there," Brian said motioning towards the back of the coach.

Just then AJ and the other passengers got out of the coach and looked up at the three men up top. One of the passengers was a woman and when Brain looked down and saw her, a huge smile came to his face. It was one of the gals he'd escorted into San Antonio; one of the 'working' girls.

"BJ...is that you up there," the woman asked with a quizzical gaze?

"Annie? Well, I'll be hanged...it is you. How've you been," Brian said as he climbed down off the top of the coach?

When he was on the ground, Annie gave him a big hug and looked up at him, "You don't know how good it is to see you again. You must be my guardian angel, honey. Every time I get in trouble you show up to save me," Annie said happily.

"It looks that way, doesn't it? What brings you up this way," Brian asked?

"After you left us down in San Antonio, I ran into my long lost brother while shopping one day. He told me he and his wife had a store up here in Abilene and wanted me to come and help them with their business. I grabbed the opportunity to change lifestyles, so here I am...and here you are," Annie said with another wide smile.

"Aren't you going to introduce me to your lady friend," AJ asked?

"Oh, yeah...Annie, this is my brother AJ...AJ, Annie. I met Annie while I was on my way to San

Antonio; her and her traveling companions were attacked by some desperados and I stepped in to help them out," Brian said modestly.

"He's a regular hero in my books," Annie said.

"Yeah, I can see that," AJ said with a smile, "In fact, he's a legend in his own mind."

"Hey...I resemble that remark," Brian said with a laugh.

"Well, folks, I hate to break this reunion up, but I've got to get this coach on up to Abilene," the driver stated apologetically.

"Yeah, sure...we understand that," AJ said getting an agreeing nod from Brian.

The passengers started to re-board the coach and the guard and driver climbed back up top while AJ and Brian untied their mounts from the back of the coach. As Brian was stepping up on his horse he looked up the hill and saw the cavalry troop just topping it.

"Looks like the cavalry arrived a little late," Brian said causing the others to look in the cavalry's direction.

The detail rode up to the coach and the lieutenant gave a slight salute. He looked passed the coach at the dead bodies of the Indians and commented, "Looks like we're a little late to the party."

"Yeah, you missed a real wingding of one," AJ grinned.

"These men saved us from being bushwhacked," the driver called down.

"Which way did the others go," the lieutenant asked?

"They headed down the road in that direction," Brian said and then added. "There were a few Comancheros joined them after the melee. I saw them ride out of those rocks down there."

"Thanks again. You Sackett's are a real boon to the people around here, I'd have to say," the lieutenant said with a smile and then looked back and gave the command to follow him.

The troopers rode off in search of the remaining renegade Comanche's and the coach got started on its way to Abilene. Brian and AJ followed along for about six miles and then cut cross country towards the Sackett ranch.

Chapter 10

SHERIFF DAWSON and his posse had given up the chase of Black Jack Haggerty and Four Fingers Jordan after four days of hard riding. They had almost caught up to the two, but lost their tracks when the two outlaws ran across a herd of wild horses. The two bandits had mingled in with the herd causing the posse to lose their trail. This ploy, when the opportunity presented itself, was used often by men on the run.

The sheriff walked into the saloon and sat down heavily in a chair at a table near the door. He was tired and it showed in his face. He waved at the bartender and called out, "A cold one over here, Bob."

The bartender drew a mug of beer and carried it over to the sheriff. He grinned as he sat the beer in front of the aging lawman.

"Getting a little tougher to go out on them four day posse rides, eh, Gray?"

"It's always been tough, Bob. You should try it sometime. I tell you, them boys did every trick in the book and finally hit the big one when they ran across a herd of wild horses. There ain't no one could track two men in a herd the size of that one," the sheriff came back.

"Did Harmon tell you about the man and woman over at the doc's place there? They had a run in with the two bank robbers and the man was seriously wounded," the bartender asked?

"No, he didn't. I swear I would fire that good for nothing deputy of mine if he wasn't my brother in law. You say they're over at the doc's place," the sheriff asked with a frown?

"Have been for several days; in fact, they arrived the day before Jim Chauncey killed Abe Hartman," the bartender stated.

"What? What do you mean, 'the day before Chauncey killed Abe Hartman?'"

"You mean to tell me that Harmon didn't tell you about the shooting either? I see what you mean about him being worthless. Yeah, Abe drew on Chauncey and his gun misfired and Jim killed him. It was a pure case of self defense, but you'd think your deputy would have said something," Bob chuckled.

"That does it; wife or no wife, I'm going to fire that no good lazy pole cat as soon as I get back to the office. But, first I'll stop by the doctor's and check on this hombre the bank robbers shot," the sheriff stated.

"That'll be a nickel, Gray," the bartender said, reminding the sheriff he hadn't paid for his beer.

"Put it on my bill. The city will settle up at the end of the month," the sheriff said, causing the bartender to walk away mumbling to himself.

THE SHERIFF walked across the street and into the doctor's office. The doc was just coming out of his small operating room where he'd removed a boil off a cowboy's neck.

"Say, Doc, how goes it," the sheriff asked cordially?

"Not bad at all, Gray; how did your posse make out," the doctor asked?

"We didn't catch 'em, if that's what you mean. I hear you had to patch up someone who ran into the holdup men, is that right," the sheriff asked?

"I did at that. He was in bad shape when I got to him, but he pulled through and I think he's gonna be just fine," the doctor stated.

"Where do you have him now?"

"Oh, I have him in my side room; I call it my extended stay recovery room," the doctor chuckled.

"Can I talk to him," the sheriff asked?

"I don't see why not; he's up to it, I'm sure," the doctor said and then added, "But don't question him too long or hard."

"No, no, I just want to ask him a couple of questions about the men who shot him," the sheriff said holding his hand up.

The doctor went with the sheriff and opened the door to the room where he had Brent recuperating. When they opened the door the doctor noticed that Brent was asleep and started to tell the sheriff to wait until his patient was awake. Before he could convey his request to the sheriff, the lawman reached out and shook Brent's shoulder gently.

When Brent opened his eyes, the first thing he saw was a shiny badge pinned on the sheriff's vest. Brent's eyes widened and he pulled the pistol out from under the pillow and fired before either the doctor or the sheriff knew what was happening.

The bullet hit the sheriff in the right shoulder, spinning him around and knocking him back against the wall. He hit his head hard enough to knock himself out.

"What are you doing," the doctor yelled out as he turned out of shear reflex to attend to the sheriff.

Brent's eyes were wide and held a wild look as he fired one more time; this bullet hitting the doctor in the back. The doctor went to the floor in a heap.

The gunshots brought Julia running, along with a young woman who worked part time for the doctor. Julia stopped in her tracks when she saw what Brent had done.

Brent still looked crazed, having been roused from a terrible dream he had been having. A dream that had him being cornered by a huge posse that wanted nothing less than to hang him.

"Brent, Brent...oh, what have you done," Julia said holding Brent to her bosom.

"What, what...," Brent stammered shaking his head to clear his thoughts..

He looked at the gun in his hand and then at Julia. Only then did he realize what he had just done.

"Oh, my god...what did I do? I thought...," Brent said as the young part time nurse went into hysterics.

"You shot the doctor and the sheriff," she began screaming.

"Come on, we've got to get out of here," Julia said as she began trying to get Brent out of the bed.

The young nurse was still screaming and Julia had no other recourse than to slap the woman as hard as she could. The woman stopped screaming, but ran out of the room and into the street.

With Brent's help Julia was able to get him out the back door of the doctor's office and into the wagon. Julia looked at Brent as her man now, and her duty was to see that he got away from here as soon as possible.

The young nurse ran down the middle of the street muttering that the doctor and sheriff had been shot. While she was doing that, Julia was driving the wagon out of town, whipping the horses into a gallop.

This jostling around was not going to be good for Brent, but Julia had to put as much distance between them and the town as possible. Brent lay in the bed that Julia had made for herself while he was being treated by the doctor.

Julia didn't know her way around the area, but she did know the road was no place to be. She'd have to find a place to get off the main road and then find a place where they could lay low for awhile.

Deputy Sheriff Dudley Harmon formed a small posse and set out in pursuit of Brent and Julia. He had never ridden in a posse before, much less led one, and it showed. He had them following the wrong set of wagon tracks from the outset and wound up at a homesteader's place two miles in the opposite direction of that which Julia and Brent had headed.

Julia found a grove of trees that would offer them cover while she checked on Brent's condition. Fortunately the jostling hadn't reopened the wound. She looked at Brent wonderingly and he forced a half grin and shook his head negatively.

"I don't know what to say, Julia. I woke up and saw a man hovering over me wearing a badge and I lost it. I thought he was there to kill me. I just started shooting and couldn't stop," he said.

"What do we do now, Brent; tell me, because I don't know," Julia said with a pleading look on her face?

Brent thought for a moment as to the best solution to the situation he had forced upon them. He gave Julia a serious look once he'd made up his mind.

"You've got to take me back to Sundown and turn me over to the law. I won't let you ruin your life over my actions. It's the only thing we can do," Brent said as he thought it out.

"I don't want to lose you, Brent. We can do something. I know, we can go to California.

Nobody would know us out there. We'll start over a fresh," Julia argued.

"It won't work, Julia. It would only be a matter of time and my name and face would be known to the lawmen out there. No, you've got to take me back to Sundown," Brent said with finality in his voice.

Julia looked at him for several long, tortured moments before slowly nodding in agreement with Brent's orders.

Raymond D. Mason

Chapter 11

THE FOLKS of Sundown were all abuzz about the shootings of the sheriff and the only doctor in town. Emotions were running at fever pitch. The young woman who had witnessed the shootings had suffered a mental breakdown and was making little sense at all. She kept repeating over and over, "He shot them both."

Julia drove the wagon back into town and pulled up in front of the sheriff's office. She expected the deputy sheriff to come out and arrest Brent immediately and was taken aback when she looked in the office and saw no one there.

"There's no one inside, Brent. What should I do," Julia asked?

"They're probably out looking for me. I'm sure the young nurse alerted the town to what happened," Brent said as things began to swim before his eyes. "I'm feeling...I'm feeling," he said and blacked out.

Julia quickly climbed into the wagon and felt his pulse. His heart beat was strong; it must have been all the excitement; that, and the fact he was still weak from his wound and operation.

Looking down the street Julia saw two men riding into town and wondered if they were members of the posse. She had to get some water to try and bring Brent around so she climbed down and hurried to the nearest watering trough where she soaked a handkerchief.

The two men didn't seem to be paying much attention to the wagon, so Julia figured they were not part of the posse. What she didn't know was that these two men were Texas Rangers, and they were there because of the bank robbery they'd heard about while in Lubbock.

Julia hurried back to the wagon and began to swab Brent's face with the wet hanky. He opened his eyes and looked up at her.

"I must have dozed off," he said.

"I've got to get you some help, Dan. You need to get your strength back," Julia replied.

"Don't call me Dan...call me Brent. I've been someone else long enough. I won't use Sackett though, because I don't want to smear the family name," Brent said and then had a thought.

"Julia, let's get out of town. I know what I have to do. I want you to take me to Abilene. I've got to make amends with my family. Once I've done that,

Ride the Hard Land

then I'm going to turn myself in to the sheriff there."

"Are you sure that's what you want to do?"

"Yeah, it is. I've got to see my family again. I think it's time for me to mend some fences," Brent said thoughtfully.

Julia smiled lovingly at the man she had fallen in love with as she tenderly touched Brent's face. The sound of the man's voice next to the wagon gave her a start, causing her to pull her hand back quickly.

"Are you all right in there," the man asked.

It was Dudley Harmon, the deputy sheriff?

"Oh, yes," Julia said wide eyed. "I was just tending to my husband," she said.

"What's wrong with him," Harmon asked?

"He was injured some time ago and he felt a little weak. Are you the sheriff," Julia asked, pretending to just be passing through.

"No, well...yeah, I guess I am...now. You see someone shot the sheriff and the town's only doctor. I've been out with a posse trying to run them down, but we lost their trail. We just rode back into town," Harmon said and gave Julia a curious look before going on.

"Haven't I seen you before," Harmon asked? "You look mighty familiar."

"Oh, you may have seen me in one of the stores. We were camped outside of town and I had to come in for supplies," Julia said innocently.

"Yeah, that must be it. I never forget a face. I ain't too good on names, but faces I'm good at," Harmon stated.

81

Raymond D. Mason

"We'll be moving on as soon as I get something for us to eat," Julia said with a smile.

"Oh, then you want to go to the café down the street there. They have good grub," Harmon said, pointing in the direction of the café.

"I meant groceries," Julia smiled and then asked, "You said someone shot the sheriff and the doctor? Who was it; do you know?"

"No, the young gal that witnessed it has had some kind of breakdown and hasn't told us very much. She just keeps saying 'He shot them'.

"The sheriff was shot in the shoulder and knocked unconscious. The doctor was shot in the back, but he's still hanging on to life. We sent a telegram to Lubbock to get a doctor out here. Hopefully he'll make it before our doctor dies. There's a woman who works as a midwife sometimes tending to both the doctor and the sheriff now," Harmon stated taking on an air of authority.

"I see," Julia said, somewhat relieved that both men were still alive, but knowing that either man could identify Brent as the shooter.

"Well, I'd better get over to the doctor's office and check on them. You folks have a safe journey to...where'd you say you were headed," Harmon asked?

"I didn't, but it's...San Antonio," Julia lied.

Harmon nodded and gave a friendly grin as the two men Julia had seen earlier rode up to where they were.

"We hear the sheriff was shot and you're the man in charge here now, is that right," one of the men asked?

"Yep, what can I do for you..., Ranger," Harmon said as he noticed the Texas Ranger badges the men were wearing.

"We've got a few questions we'd like to ask you," the first ranger said.

Julia took this as a convenient opportunity to leave.

"We really have to be going. Thank you for your help," she said, looking quickly from Harmon to the rangers.

"Adios, Ma'am; have a safe trip," Harmon said and tipped his hat as she drove away.

Julia looked back inside the wagon at Brent and stated, "They're both alive, Brent. Thank God you didn't kill either of them."

Brent looked up at Julia and replied, "It sounds like the doctor is in bad shape though. I hope he pulls through."

"They don't know it was you who shot them, Brent; let's leave town now...this is our chance to get away clean," Julia pleaded once again.

"Well, we can go somewhere so I can heal up and then I'll decide if we're going to Abilene or not. Let's go to the ranch you and your husband bought. I can recoup there," Brent said thoughtfully.

Julia smiled widely as she grabbed the harness reins and snapped the team of horses up. They drove down through the center of town to the general store. Julia hurriedly went inside and picked up some groceries to take to the ranch.

While she shopped she prayed the doctor would live, but with mixed feelings. He was the one who could identify the shooter by name...if he hadn't done so already.

Chapter 12

BILL NUGENT and his wife arrived in Abilene and drove their wagon around in back of the Feed and Grain Store. Nugent went inside the store and his wife went to do their tri-monthly shopping at the various stores around town.

Jim Chauncey rode slowly down Abilene's main street looking from side to side and tipping his hat to every woman he saw. Because of the two men he'd killed in gun fights Chauncey was feeling cock sure of himself and had taken on an air of arrogance. After all, the two men he'd taken down both had reputations as being handy with a gun.

When Chauncey saw Tanya Nugent walking down the street a grin pulled at the corner of his mouth. He reined his horse to the hitching rail in front of the Abilene Emporium and General Merchandise Store.

Tanya glanced at the handsome Chauncey and he tipped his hat to her just before she reached the front door of the store. When she went inside the building, Chauncey beat the dust from his clothes with his hat before entering the store himself.

He didn't pretend to be in the store for any other reason than meeting the woman he'd just seen. When he saw her looking at a bolt of material he headed in that direction.

"I can make you a real good deal on that material," Chauncey said as he walked up to Tanya.

Tanya looked at him and smiled slightly, "Oh, do you work here?"

"No...that's why I can make you a good deal on that material. I'll buy it for you if you'll promise to make me a shirt out of it," Chauncey said seriously.

"I don't know you and I don't think you'd want to ride all the way down to where we live to pick it up," Tanya said, somewhat amused by Chauncey's approach.

"Honey, I'd go to the ends of the earth just to spend one hour with you."

"Oh, is that right. Well, when you got to the end of the earth you'd find my husband waiting for you," Tanya said, letting this saddle sore lothario know she was married.

"Husbands have never been a problem I couldn't handle. In fact, I prefer my women to be married," Chauncey went on with his line.

"Oh, is that right? Well, there's one thing that I'm not," Mrs. Nugent said, still with a faint smile.

"Oh, and what's that?"

Ride the Hard Land

"I'm not one of your women...and what's more... I will never be one of your women. Do I make myself clear, sir?"

"Oh you make yourself clear, but I don't believe you. You see, I'm the best when it comes to reading a woman's eyes. Now take you for instance; your words say one thing, but your eyes are saying something totally different," Chauncey said with a smirk.

"If you don't mind, I've got more important things to do than stand here talking to you...a complete stranger," Mrs. Nugent said.

"That's right; we haven't been introduced, have we. My name is Jim Chauncey. I'm pleased to make your acquaintance Mrs. ...?"

"Mrs. Nobody, to you. Now if you'll excuse me I have some shopping to do," Mrs. Nugent said and turned to go.

Chauncey let out a laugh and patted Mrs. Nugent on the derriere. Instantly Mrs. Nugent spun around and slapped Chauncey in the face as hard as she could. The suddenness of the blow flew all over Chauncey.

An automatic reflex caused Chauncey to counter Mrs. Nugent attack and he hit her across the face with the back of his hand. Several people in the store saw what had happened, but no one came to Mrs. Nugent's defense; not even the store owner when a customer complained.

"It's a family matter, I'm sure," the store owner said quickly.

"I don't think so. I saw her and another man enter town in a wagon earlier. Aren't you even going to question him," the woman customer asked?

"That's for the sheriff to do, not me. Excuse me, I see another customer who needs some assistance," the owner said and hurried towards another female customer.

Tanya Nugent put her hand to her face. She saw blood on the back of her hand when she removed it from her cheek. Chauncey frowned deeply as he turned and headed for the door. As he opened the door to go, another man was just entering. The two of them stood staring at one another for a moment before Chauncey moved on. The man entering the store was Bill Nugent.

From several yards away Nugent could see the redness on his wife's cheek. He also saw the look in her eyes as he walked up to her.

"Are you all right, honey," Nugent asked?

Tanya lowered her eyes as she spoke, "It's nothing, Bill...let's just let it go."

"No, I won't let it go," Nugent said as he walked up to where Tanya was standing. "What happened here? Why is your cheek so red...and why is there blood in the corner of your mouth?"

Just then a woman standing near the Nugent's spoke up, "That man you met in the doorway when you came in slapped your wife."

Nugent cast a quick, angry look towards the woman as he snapped back, "He slapped her?"

"Yes, when your wife tried to ignore his advances he patted her on her...let's say, behind. When she turned and slapped him is when he hit her," the woman went on.

Nugent didn't ask anymore questions. He stalked across the room to the front door and stepped out onto the boardwalk. Looking up and down the street he finally saw the man he was looking for; and he was going into a nearby saloon.

Nugent adjusted the gun belt on his hip as he started for the saloon. He knew the pistol was loaded; he'd checked it just before they were attacked by the Comanche renegades and all he'd used against them was his rifle.

The saloon was well over half full as Nugent pushed the doors open and looked around for the man who'd entered a few moments before him. When he spotted Chauncey just sitting down at a table he called out to him. Nugent walked across the room and stopped in front of Chauncey.

"You slapped my wife and I'm going to kill you," Nugent said with a piercing glare.

Chauncey looked up at the man who'd just threatened him and nodded slowly as he muttered, "Is that right?"

"Yeah, that's right. She was the 'lady' in the Emporium that you just left. Now get up and fill your hand," Nugent said with clenched teeth.

"If I get up I'm going to kill you. Maybe you don't know who you're messing with? My name is Jim Chauncey. Are you still as anxious to do battle with me," Chauncey said arrogantly.

"Your name means nothing to me. Get up," Nugent repeated.

"Okay, you ask for it...get ready to die," Chauncey said as he started to get up but went for his gun at the same time.

Nugent wasn't fooled by the move and drew and fired before Chauncey had his gun halfway out of its holster. The roar echoed around the big room and the smell of spent gunpowder filled the air. Chauncey fell backwards across a table behind him and then rolled off onto the floor.

Nugent looked around the room and saw the gawking faces of the witnesses. He didn't have to say a word; the crowd began saying that the dead man had been the one to draw first.

"Someone go for the sheriff," the bartender yelled out.

A young boy who had witnessed the shooting from start to finish by watching it from under the batwing doors called out, "I'll go."

The boy broke down the street in a dead run. When he reached the sheriff's office he ran through the door and told the sheriff what had happened. The sheriff jumped to his feet and followed the young lad back to the saloon.

Nugent was still standing there, waiting for the sheriff. The sheriff stopped and looked down at the dead man. He looked quickly back at Nugent.

"This man has been in a couple of shootouts over the past couple of days and came out on top, from what I hear. His name is Jim Chauncey; does that name mean anything to you," the sheriff asked?

"It doesn't mean a thing to me; he insulted my wife and then slapped her; that is all I know about him. I told him I was going to kill him and he tried to get me first. That's all there is to it," Nugent replied.

"How many of you saw what happened," the sheriff asked the onlookers?

"I did, Sheriff," an old timer said.

"Me too, Sam," another joined in.

The sheriff stood there for a moment and then snapped, "Well, what happened?"

"It's just like the man said. He told the man he was going to kill him; the guy went for his gun while standing up, but this fella was too fast for him," the old timer stated.

The sheriff looked at the other man who said he'd witnessed the incident and asked, "Is that the way you saw it, too?"

"Yep, just like that. To be honest I thought the dead man was going to win the fight," the other witness said.

"Get out of here. This guy might have friends," the sheriff said to Nugent.

"You're not going to hold me for a hearing or anything," Nugent queried?

"No, I know these men and they are reliable witnesses."

Nugent looked around and as he headed for the door said, "Thanks a lot, Sheriff."

The sheriff watched Nugent go and then said under his breath, "Why didn't I become a preacher?"

Raymond D. Mason

Chapter

13

BRIAN AND AJ rode slowly down the long hillside that led to the Sackett ranch house. Brian was troubled, but didn't know why. He had been experiencing a nauseous feeling for several days but hadn't let on to AJ about it. He felt it had something to do with Brent.

"Hey, it'll be good to get some home cooking, eh, Brian," AJ said with a grin.

"You said it. My cooking was beginning to make me a might ill," Brian replied as they neared the front gate to the yard.

"You and me both," AJ laughed.

AJ noticed two horses tied at the hitching rail in front of the house. He didn't recognize either horse, knowing the horses that all the ranch hands rode; none of them rode a palomino or paint.

"Looks like we have visitors," AJ commented to Brian as they rode up alongside the horses at the rail.

"Yeah," Brian answered as they both stepped down off their mounts and tied them to the rail also.

When they entered the house they were greeted by their pa who instantly introduced them to the US Marshal and his deputy.

Ignoring the men with their father, AJ said quickly, "Hi there; Pa, we have Abner's body tied on his horse outside."

"What? Abner is dead...how," John Sackett asked?

"Comanche's," AJ replied.

"What's this? I take it the dead man is one of your ranch hands," the marshal asked?

"AJ, Brian, this is Marshal Ben Coyle and his deputy Martin Bloom. They're looking for Brent. They say he's wanted for robbery and murder. You're the last one of the family to have seen him, what do you know about this," John asked pointedly with a deep frown on his face?

AJ replied quickly hoping to deflect the questions away from Brian, "Yes, marshal; the dead man's name is Abner Sikes; he worked for us. We had sent him out to Possum Creek. That's where we found his body."

Brian looked from AJ to his pa and then to the marshal and his deputy and then answered.

"Yeah, Pa...he told me all about it when we met up in San Antonio," Brian answered.

Ride the Hard Land

"Why didn't you tell us that he was on the run from the law," John asked with a frown?

"I didn't want to upset you all with the bad news. I planned on doing it when the time was right," Brian said.

"Well, I guess the time is right now, huh," John replied.

Brian nodded slowly and then asked the marshal, "What are you doing here? He isn't here if that's what you're thinking."

"We think he might be heading for Abilene and if he is then this would be the most likely place he'd show up. I hope you don't cross the line and try to hide him out. That would make you guilty of aiding and abetting a criminal," the marshal said locking his gaze on Brian.

"He didn't act like he was the least bit interested in returning home when I talked to him," Brian stated honestly.

"He's going by the name Dan Johnson, or at least he was. If you should make contact with him, it would be better for all concerned if you notified Sheriff Shelby. We'll be staying in town for a few days so the sheriff could let us know and we'll come back out," the marshal said looking from one Sackett to the next.

"You're asking us to do a lot, Marshal," John said. "Brent is still my son, after all. I won't turn him in and I doubt that either of his brothers will either."

"We'll get Brent sooner or later. I hope you won't make this any harder on yourselves than it all ready is," the marshal said seriously.

"I hope we don't either," John replied.

"Come on Martin, I guess we've done about all we can for now. Have a good day," the marshal said and the two of them walked to the door.

As the two men started out the marshal looked back and offered, "I know this is a hard thing for you to be faced with, but I've seen some of the family members of the people that Brent killed. It was hard for them, too."

The marshal and his deputy mounted up with John, AJ, and Brian standing on the porch and watching them. Once the lawmen had rode away John spoke.

"We're going to find Brent before the law does. I can't stand idly by and watch him hunted down by a posse. We've got to find him and get him down to Mexico. I want you two to locate him," John stated.

"Okay, Pa. I'd say we go back to San Antonio and start there since that's where I ran into him," Brian said.

"We'll head out first thing tomorrow morning," AJ said firmly.

"I know this will be harder on you, Brian, seeing as how you just got back from your long ride down that way; but you've got a better handle on what Brent might do than any of the rest of us. You and him think alike as well as look alike. I've always said if you cut one the other one bleeds," John said with a slight grin.

"Okay, Pa, but we'll need to take some money for Brent. He may not have any to live on once we find him and get him south of the border," Brian said.

Ride the Hard Land

AJ added, "We'll each take an extra horse, too. We can cover at least an extra ten to fifteen miles a day by having a fresher horse to switch to."

"Yes, you're right. I have a little over three thousand dollars here at the ranch that you can take. I don't want to go in to Abilene and take it from the bank. That marshal and his deputy probably have given the bank orders to inform them of any large withdrawals from our account," John said.

"Tomorrow it is then," Brian said resignedly.

The truth was that Brian had been so pleased to get back to the ranch that he wasn't looking forward to the long ride in search of Brent. He knew, however, that it was the right thing to do, so that's the way it would be. At least he would have AJ along on this trip.

JULIA DROVE the wagon around in back of the house where she and Brent would be staying. It was definitely out of the way, so she didn't figure too many people would be passing by.

She managed to get Brent inside the house and while he rested she began unloading what few things there was in the wagon. Once she got some blankets down on the floor she lay Brent down and checked to make sure the jostling around hadn't reopened his wounds.

Julia had to cut some wood to build a fire, but soon had a fire going and was cooking supper. Brent watched her and pondered their next move. He had to bring an end to the constant running from the law, but how?

As he watched her busy making them something to eat he thought of her late husband and how his life had come to an abrupt end. Suddenly his eyes brightened as he had a thought. That was the answer to their problem; his life ending abruptly.

The more he thought about it, the more the thought took on substance. It would have to wait until he was strong enough to carry it out, but the wait shouldn't be all that long.

A smile made its way to his face as he thought about the plan. Julia glanced his way and smiled.

"What are you smiling about? Are you watching me," she asked?

"Yep, I sure am. And I think I have a way out of our situation. I'll tell you about it once I have all the details worked out. I think you'll like it," Brent said confidently.

"Do you mean without you having to give yourself up," Julia asked?

"Yes. This will be better for everyone concerned," Brent smiled.

Chapter 14

BRIAN AND AJ left the ranch early the next morning. They each led an extra horse, and AJ also led a pack animal. They decided to make a stop in Abilene and pick up a few more cartridges for their pistols and Winchesters.

They planned to go into the General Store through the back door to avoid being seen by the marshal that was looking for Brent. It was fortunate for them that they made the stop.

The two brothers rode down a small alleyway behind the General Store and tied up to an unhitched buckboard. They went through the back door and walked towards the front of the store.

The store owner had just came downstairs from the family's quarters above the store and unlocked the back door. He was still in the storeroom and the presence of AJ and Brian startled him.

"Oh, my lord, boys...you gave me quite a fright. I didn't realize anyone had come in yet," the owner said.

"Sorry about that Ben; we just stopped by to buy some cartridges and decided to tie up out back," AJ apologized.

"Whew...sure thing; what do you need," Ben said as the three moved out into the store.

Just then someone tried the front door and found it locked since Ben had not had a chance to unlock it yet. He hurried to the door and quickly opened up for business. The customer was a man by the name of Homer Crandall.

"Well, howdy Homer. How was your trip from Clovis, New Mexico? Did you get your sister moved out there all right," Ben asked his customer?

"Yeah, it went all right. Our littlest one came down with a case of tonsillitis and was running a fever, but other than that, no trouble at all," Homer said as he and Ben walked towards the middle of the store.

Homer needed a couple of items and had decided to stop on their way home to pick them up. He walked by AJ and Brian who were looking at guns in a glass case.

As Ben got past them he stopped and turned around and gave Brian a long stare. Brian noticed and commented.

"Is there something wrong," Brian asked?

"No, no...it's just that...weren't you in the town of Sundown about five days ago," Homer asked Brian?

"Sundown...no...why," Brian asked?

Ride the Hard Land

"I swear I saw a man in the doctor's office there that looked exactly like you. Come to think of it, it couldn't have been you; that man was in too bad of shape to have beat me here," Homer said thoughtfully.

"And this was five days ago," AJ quickly asked?

"Uh, huh; five days ago," Homer stated firmly.

AJ and Brian looked at one another and nodded slowly. They wouldn't be heading south after all. They'd be heading northwest to a small town called Sundown.

The ride to Sweetwater was a good day's ride and by the time they arrived there it was nearing sundown. They made camp just the other side of town and after supper both men went right to sleep. The next morning they feasted on biscuits their sister had sent along with them and were in the saddle before sunup.

They made the town of Snyder the next day and heard that the town had a hard case for a sheriff. He ran the town with an iron fist and a fast gun. He had a couple of businesses in town and had a definite drinking problem. His name was Clyde Rule.

Brian and AJ had decided to spend the night in a hotel and sleep in a real bed. Upon arriving in town they tied up in front of the Snyder Hotel, owned by Sheriff Rule. Before entering the building they beat the dust off their pants and shirt using their hats. When they walked up to the desk the clerk looked up and smiled.

"I take it you're here for the hanging," the clerk said happily.

"Hanging...no we're just passing through," AJ said. "When's the hanging?"

"Tomorrow at two o'clock. The hangman is in town all ready. Right up them stairs," the clerk said motioning towards the staircase.

"Is that right? Well, we just want a room," AJ stated.

"You are in luck, gentlemen. I have one room left. I tell you, folks are coming from all around to watch this hanging," the clerk said with a wide grin.

"Who is it that's getting hanged? Not that we'd know them, mind you," Brian asked with a grin?

"It's none other than Frank 'Four Fingers' Jordan. Yep, the sheriff has him locked up over in the jail right this instant," the clerk said nodding his head excitedly.

AJ looked quickly at Brian, "Four Fingers Jordan? I don't suppose Black Jack Haggerty was caught also?"

"No, but the sheriff caught Jordan. He just walked up behind him in the saloon and cold cocked him as big as you please. The bartender had recognized him and sent word to the sheriff that Jordan was in the saloon. We have a sheriff that no one messes with if they know what's good for them."

"Is that right," Brian replied.

A voice from behind them caused them to turn and look in the man's direction who spoke the words, "That's right."

Brian noticed the badge first and commented, "Oh, hello Sheriff. So you caught Four Fingers Jordan, huh?"

"I did. Do you know him, by any chance?"

"We don't know him, but Jordan and the Haggerty gang attacked our ranch a few months back. I'd say if Jordan was here in town Haggerty couldn't be too far away," AJ responded.

"Where'd this attack take place," the sheriff asked?

"Back at our ranch in Abilene; the Sackett spread," AJ answered.

"Sackett...I have a poster on a Brent Sackett. He wouldn't be kin to you would he?"

"He would. He's our brother," Brian answered.

The sheriff gave both men a hard glare and glanced at their side arms. It wasn't hard to see what the sheriff was thinking.

"No, we're not running from the law, Sheriff," AJ said evenly.

"That paper I have on Brent doesn't have a photograph on it, but the description sure fits you," the sheriff said looking at Brian.

"It should, Brent's my twin brother. Didn't the wanted poster say anything about that fact," Brian snapped?

"Yeah, come to think about it, it did say something like that," the sheriff replied. "So do you have any idea where your brother might be?"

"Nope, he never came home after the War. We fought on different sides," Brian said truthfully.

"I won't ask which side you fought on," the sheriff frowned and then asked, "You boys planning on sticking around for the hanging tomorrow?"

"We had thought about staying an extra day, but, I don't think so now. I'm not one who likes to watch a hanging. I've seen two and that's enough for me," AJ replied and then added, "We'll be riding on in the morning."

"It ain't everyday you get to see someone as famous as Four Fingers Jordan get his neck stretched, though," the sheriff grinned crookedly.

"I guess not, huh. But we'll pass," AJ restated his previous intention.

"Well, I'll let you boys get on up to your room. Keep your noses clean while you're in my town and we'll get along real fine," the sheriff said as his eyes narrowed.

"That's what we're planning on doing," Brian said.

With that, the sheriff turned and walked out the front door of the hotel. Brian and AJ stood and watched him go and then looked at one another.

"It looks like this town has a sheriff who means business," AJ said with a slight grin.

"That it does, brother, that it does," Brian agreed.

The sheriff returned to his office and checked on his two prisoners; one being Four Fingers Jordan. He grinned when Jordan looked up at him as he peered through the door that separated the jail from the office.

"You'd better get a good night's sleep, Jordan. You'll be dancing on air tomorrow afternoon. I want you to be nice and fresh," the sheriff taunted.

"You ain't hung me yet, Sheriff. Remember, it ain't over until the trap door opens and I drop through it," Jordan snapped.

"You're still thinking Haggerty will be able to keep you from hanging, eh? Well, I've got news for you. He ain't coming," the sheriff said with a laugh.

Four Fingers grinned slightly as the sheriff walked up to the jail cell that contained Jordan. The sheriff frowned slightly as he studied the arrogant grin on Jordan's face.

"How do you know that Haggerty hasn't all ready been here," Jordan said as he slowly got to his feet?

The sheriff started to say something but stopped in mid sentence when Jordan pulled a pistol out from behind him and cocked the hammer back. The sheriff froze.

"What the...," the sheriff said with a frown.

"Now don't do anything stupid, Sheriff and you'll live to see another sunrise. Open this cell door...now," Jordan snapped.

"Where'd you get that gun," the sheriff demanded to know?

"Never mind, just feel fortunate that I'm in a good mood right now. If I wasn't I'd plug you where you stand," Jordan said as the sheriff slowly opened the cell door.

Jordan grabbed the sheriff by the front of the shirt and pulled him inside the cell as he stepped around him. Jordan took the sheriff's gun then shoved him hard into the cell. Standing outside the cell, Jordan closed the door and locked it.

"Let me out of here," the other prisoner called out.

"Sure thing," Jordan said as he walked over and unlocked the door to the man's cell.

"You'll never get away with this Jordan," the sheriff said without thinking.

"Oh, yeah; well if you think I'm going to just wait around until they slip that noose around my neck, you're dumber than you look," Jordan growled back.

"You still haven't told me how you got that gun," the sheriff said.

"And I ain't going to tell you. See if you can't figure it out for yourself. Now I've got to run. Adios," Jordan said as he turned and walked out into the outer office.

Jordan walked to the sheriff's desk and opened the bottom drawer. He removed his gun and gun belt and dropped the sheriff's gun into the opened drawer. He looked at the wall rack and grinned when he saw a new looking Winchester.

Unlocking the bar that held the rifles and shotguns in place, Jordan took the newer model Winchester out and held it up to his shoulder.

"Well, I don't think the sheriff will mind my taking this. I sure don't want it to burn up in the fire," Jordan said to himself.

With that, Jordan grabbed one of the coal oil lamps and threw it against the wall. He took the second lamp and threw it against the opposite wall. He walked to the front door and struck a match he removed from his shirt pocket. He grinned as he flipped the lit match towards the coal oil.

The flames shot up the far wall separating the cells from the office. Jordan lit another match and dropped it where he'd dumped the oil from the second lamp. The wall at the front of the sheriff's office began to burn also.

Jordan casually walked out to the hitching rail in front of the sheriff's office and untied a horse that was tied there. He mounted up as flames from the fire caused an orange glow through the lone front window.

Jordan looked back and smiled as he kicked the sheriff's horse he'd just stolen into a full gallop out of town. As Jordan rode by the structure that had been erected for the hanging he let out a loud whoop.

"Better luck next time, Hangman," Jordan yelled at the top of his lungs.

Raymond D. Mason

Chapter 15

FRANK JORDAN reined his horse down into the arroyo where Black Jack Haggerty was waiting for him. The two men greeted each other with a laugh as Haggerty stated, "Well, so much for a hanging, eh, partner? Did you plug that lousy sheriff?"

"No, I didn't. I let him get a taste of hell before he went there. I burned the jail down with him in it, Jordan laughed.

"You're kidding; that ought to slow a posse down from gettin' on our trail. Good thinking, Frank," Haggerty said with a frown.

"That gun on a line idea of yours worked like a charm, Jack," Jordan said.

"Well, we'd better vamoose out of here. Once they get the fire put out they'll have a posse after us, you can be sure of that," Haggerty said and then noticed the red spot on Jordan's shirt.

"It looks like you reopened that bullet wound to your shoulder, Frank," Haggerty said nodding towards the wounded area.

"Yeah, when I jumped up to grab hold of the bars, I guess. It hurts some, but it'll be okay," Jordan replied.

"We'll head down to San Antone. You can have Doc Trimble take a look at it when we get down there. That is, if he hasn't gotten himself hanged. I swear that is the most crooked man I've ever seen. He'd steal the gold out of his mother's teeth," Haggerty said with a laugh.

"Ain't it the truth," Jordan replied.

Brian and AJ were awakened by the noise of people running and hollering in the street outside the hotel. They both jumped up and looked out the window.

"There's a fire down the street...it looks like it might be at the sheriff's office," AJ said.

"As dry as everything is, this whole town could go up in smoke," Brian replied.

"What time is it, Brian do you know?"

Brian grabbed his trousers and pulled out a pocket watch, "It's two a.m.! What a lousy time for a fire."

"We'd better watch and make sure the fire doesn't jump to buildings on this side of the street," AJ said and then added, "You can take first watch."

"Me, why not you," Brian argued.

"I'm older and need more rest," AJ said and climbed back in bed.

"Thirty minutes, that's all I'm going to watch. If it ain't out by then, I'm waking you up," Brian said seriously.

"Goodnight, little brother," AJ said as he fluffed his pillow and made himself comfortable.

The townspeople were able to get the fire put out without the sheriff and his lone prisoner getting burned up. The sheriff formed a posse and lit out in pursuit of Four Fingers Jordan.

Brian and AJ were up and on the trail to Sundown by six o'clock that morning. They moved at a good pace for a good thirty miles and made camp just south of Justiceburg.

Finding a good camp site they tethered their horses to let them feed while they fixed themselves something to eat. They had just sat down to enjoy some pork and beans and some tortillas they had picked up in Snyder when they heard the sound of approaching horses; two horses.

Being a good twenty yards off the main trail, they weren't easily visible to passersby. Brian's horse had gotten tangled in the tether rope and he was untangling it as the two riders spotted them having their supper.

"Howdy, friend," one of the men called out as he and his sidekick reined their horses in the direction of AJ and Brian. "You wouldn't be willing to share some of that chow with a couple of hungry strangers, would you? We got jumped by a small band of Kiowa and lost our pack animal."

AJ eyed the two men suspiciously. Brian still had his back turned to the two men as he untangled the rope from around his horse's legs. AJ cast a quick glance at Brian and then back at the two strangers.

"We can share a can of pork and beans, I reckon," AJ said as he took a can from his saddlebags and began to open it with his knife.

Before he had finished opening the top of the can, Brian had finished untangling his horse and turned back towards the two strangers. The taller of the two men gave Brian a long look and then grinned.

"Dan Johnson, is that you," the man asked excitedly?

Brian looked at the man and then at AJ, "No, you have me mixed up with someone else. My name is Brian Sackett and this is my brother AJ. How'd you know Dan Johnson?"

"I met him down in San Antonio...are you sure you ain't Dan Johnson? I swear you look exactly like him," the man went on.

"Nope, I met Dan Johnson down in San Antone myself a few months back, and you're right; we do look alike," Brian answered.

"He's a good poker player, I'll tell you that. He took me for over eighty dollars."

"You know our names, but you haven't told us yours," AJ interjected.

"Oh, my name is Jim Harper and this is my deputy Bo Jennings. I'm a marshal and we're on the trail of a man who killed his wife up in

Lubbock. You ain't met anyone on the trail lately have you?"

"Nope, we spent last night in Snyder where they had Frank Jordan in jail. We heard this morning from the hotel clerk that Jordan escaped and tried to burn down the jail with the sheriff in it," Brian stated.

"Tried to; you mean the sheriff escaped," the marshal asked?

"Yep, and he was madder than an old wet hen from what we heard," Brian replied.

"Too bad they got the fire out so quickly," the marshal said giving his deputy a quick look.

"I take it you don't think much of the sheriff there," AJ said curiously?

"Nope, not at all; in fact, he's worse than some of the men he jails. I keep waiting to see his likeness on a wanted poster. It would do my heart good to go after that man," the marshal added.

AJ was standing there holding a large can of pork and beans. He had gotten so engrossed in the conversation that he'd forgotten he was holding the can.

"Oh, here you go," AJ said and tossed the can to the deputy.

"Thanks, I could eat a horse," the deputy said with a grin.

"Make it yours, we need ours," AJ joked.

"Where did this Kiowa war party jump you," Brian asked?

"About five or six miles north of here," the marshal said pointing in the direction from where they'd come. "To be honest, I think they just wanted our pack animal and whatever we were carrying on it."

"They'll do that," AJ answered.

The marshal pulled out his pocket knife and used it as a spoon to get some of the beans out of the can. He and the deputy were both using their knives. The marshal took on a thoughtful look and then stated, "Haggerty and Jordan robbed a bank up in Sundown a few days back. I wonder if Sheriff Rule knew that when he jailed Jordan?"

"I don't know, but they were going to hang him today if he hadn't escaped," Brian said.

AJ looked at Brian and then asked, "Have you been to Sundown, Marshal?"

"I've been all over this territory. There ain't a whole lot to see or do in Sundown, I can tell you that."

"That's where we're headed," AJ went on. "I sure hope we don't run into those Kiowa's. I'd hate to lose our horses."

"You'll be prime targets if they see you both leading horses like you are," the marshal said looking at the five horses grazing on the grass.

"I guess we would be at that," Brian said with a chuckle.

Chapter 16

BLACK JACK HAGGERTY looked at Frank Jordan thoughtfully. He rubbed the back of his neck as he thought about their next move. They had a lot of folding money in their saddlebags and no place to safely spend it.

Finally Haggerty broke the silence, "Frank we're going to head for Arizona. I know some folks down there that will hide us out and we can plan our next job. Are you up to the trip?"

"Yeah, I'm up to it. That is if I can get this shoulder taken care of. It's painin' me a little," Jordan said.

"We'll get a sawbones to look at it along the way, how's that?"

"Yeah, okay...where do these people of yours live," Jordan asked?

"Just out of Tucson a ways; have you ever been to Arizona?"

"Nope, ain't ever had no need to go there."

"It's not much better than Texas as far as the landscape. At least we can get the heat of the law off of us out there," Haggerty stated.

"Okay; then let's head for Arizona," Jordan replied.

The two badmen reined their horses to the west. They were near China Grove, but headed west in the direction of Big Spring, Texas.

As they rode along Haggerty kept a sharp eye out for any sign of Indians while Jordan seemed to be oblivious to anything going on around them. It was a good thing Haggerty was alert, because he spotted six Comanche's no more than a half mile away, moving in the opposite direction as he and Jordan.

The Comanche's stopped and watched the two riders, but after several long, tense seconds moved on. Jordan was never aware of their presence until Haggerty pointed it out to him.

"Frank, did you see those six Indians watching us," Haggerty snapped?

"No, where were they," Jordan asked?

"On that rise over yonder; you didn't see them?"

"No, I said. Where are they now," Jordan asked looking in the direction Haggerty had pointed?

"There gone now, but what if they'd decided to lift our scalps," Haggerty said with a frown.

"If they had I'd have seen them in time to kill 'em," Jordan said evenly.

"More like in time to take a bullet or an arrow in the back," Haggerty snapped. "Keep awake, Frank."

"Why, I've got you to do that. I'm not as spooky as you, Jack," Jordan grinned.

Meanwhile, in Tombstone, Arizona another member of the Sackett family, Lincoln (Linc) Sackett, climbed aboard a bronc he was breaking to ride.

With one man keeping the horse still by biting it's ear, Linc pulled his hat down tight on his head just before saying, "Let her go."

The man stepped away from the horse and watched as it went straight up. Linc lifted high out of the saddle, but managed to hang on when the horse came down stiff legged. The jarring motion almost knocked the wind out of the rangy cowboy.

"Yahoo," Linc's best friend yelled as he watched the top hand on the X-X ranch, ride the wild eyed mare.

The horse was a twister and sun fisher. She would spin to one side and then go up, turning her underbelly as far towards the sun as she could. No one had lasted on her for over six jumps. That was about to change.

Linc leaned as far back as he could to keep his center of gravity along the horse's spine. The more the mare bucked the more respect Linc had for her. She had the spirit and grace of a stallion. She was one of a kind in Linc's book.

Horse and rider fought one another for over two minutes. Linc could feel her tiring as well as something else. His nose was bleeding from the jarring he'd been taking.

After another thirty to forty seconds the mare stopped with her head held low and her sides heaving. She had spent ever ounce of energy she had in making the high, twisting leaps.

Linc sat atop the mare with his head down as well. He had ridden some tough broncs in his day, but this mare topped them all. He hoped he had broken her will, but not her spirit. Somehow he didn't think he had, though.

He climbed off the chestnut mare and patted her neck. She turned her head and looked at him for a moment and then brushed him with her nose. Linc gave her a loving pat and walked over to the corral railing.

"She's a good one," he said as he reached into his back pocket and pulled out a red bandana and wiped his nose.

Linc's friend, Montana, was grinning from ear to ear as he said, "I thought you were a goner a half a dozen times, Linc. How you managed to stay aboard her, I'll never know."

"Me neither, Monty; I actually tried to dismount a couple of times, but she wouldn't let me," Linc laughed.

"I hope she her gait is a lot smoother than her bucking. If it isn't everyone who rides her will wind up with nosebleeds," Monty laughed.

Linc looked back at the pretty mare and saw that she was looking in their direction. He took a deep breath and stated, "Back to work."

Ride the Hard Land

He walked over to the mare and standing to the side of her, patted her neck again. He looped the halter rope around her neck and kept it drawn taut as he slowly climbed into the saddle.

The mare stood there perfectly still for what seemed like a full five seconds. Linc didn't rush her, but let her get used to him sitting astraddle her. He felt her take a deep breath and prepared himself for another jarring ride.

Exhaling, the mare turned her head as if trying to look back at her rider. Linc let off on the tension he had been holding on the halter rope and she responded. The mare walked straight ahead, slowly and cautiously.

Linc reined her to the left and once she responded to that command he reined her to the right. Again, she responded. He could tell she was still slightly winded from the workout the two of them had endured. He wondered how she would be after she'd caught her wind.

"It looks like you've broken her will, Linc," Montana called out.

"I hope so; I can't take much more of the thumping I took earlier," Linc replied.

"I think she's just waiting for you to relax a little bit more, Linc," one of the other hands called out; a man named Latimer.

"Could be, Latimer," Linc replied to the man he'd had several run-ins with before.

"Yeah, your hind end was three feet out of the saddle most of the ride before," Latimer pushed.

"Uh huh," Linc said as he reined the mare around the corral.

"I'd venture to say that you wouldn't care to take that kind of beating again," Latimer called out, getting some hard looks from the other wranglers watching Linc.

"How long did you last on her, Latimer," Linc asked? "What was it three, four jumps?"

Latimer bristled slightly as the other men chuckled knowing he'd gone off the mare's back after two twisting leaps.

"Hey, my wrist pained me," Latimer snapped.

"Not near as much as your backside when it hit the ground," Linc said as he passed near the spot where Latimer was standing.

Without seeing it coming, Linc was taken by surprise when Latimer threw his hat under the mare. The shock of the hat sailing under her caused the mare to give one wild, twisting leap into the air, catching Linc by surprise and sending him flying off her back.

Linc landed in a cloud of dust, but was on his feet in a flash; his eyes black with anger. Linc rushed towards the spot where Latimer was standing and leaped towards the corral railing.

Linc hit Latimer with a crushing right hand to the jaw that sent the cowboy sprawling backwards off the fence. Before Latimer knew what had hit him, Linc was over the railings and sitting on Latimer's chest.

With Latimer looking up at him with glazed eyes, Linc shoved himself up off the man and came down on his stomach hard. This knocked the wind out of Latimer causing him to begin gasping for breath.

Ride the Hard Land

Linc got up and glared at the man who'd been a constant antagonist ever since Linc had hired on at the ranch. The men watching the two of them began to whoop and holler. Latimer had been the bully in the bunkhouse ever since he'd hired on a year before Linc got there.

"Oh, man; Latimer has had that coming for the longest time," a man named Stretch laughed.

"I was waiting for this to happen," another cowhand said joining in the laughter.

Linc looked back in the direction of the mare and shook his head as he muttered, "That could be a week's setback in training her. Now I've got to regain her confidence all over again."

Looking back at Latimer, who was now on his hands and knees, Linc snapped angrily, "If you ever pull a stunt like that again, Latimer I'll do more than just knock the wind out of you."

Latimer tried to respond, but nothing came out of his mouth; nothing understandable anyway. Linc called to Montana, "Give me a hand, Monty; let's get that saddle and halter rope off Scarlet."

"Scarlet...is that what you're going to name this horse," Montana asked?

"Yep; for two reasons; the first being it fits her personality. The second reason being that scarlet will be the color of the substance pouring out of Latimer's nose if he ever messes with that horse again," Linc stated.

Raymond D. Mason

Chapter 17

JESS LATIMER walked back to the bunkhouse very slowly. He had never had someone stand up to him here on the ranch before and he didn't like it. He'd get even with Linc Sackett if it was the last thing he ever did.

Latimer walked to his bunk and knelt down to retrieve the wooden box under his bed. He pulled the box out and took the oily cleaning rag from around the .44 caliber pistol inside.

He stared at the revolver for a moment before he cocked the hammer back halfway and spun the cylinder before checking to make sure the gun was loaded. Now it was his turn to embarrass Linc Sackett.

Linc and Montana had just finished taking the saddle and halter rope off the mare when Latimer walked up to the corral fence. He was holding the pistol down at his side. The men around the corral noticed and moved back.

"Sackett, I'm going to make you pay for what you did. Nobody does that to Jess Latimer and gets away with it. Now I want to see you dance," Latimer snapped with a deep frown.

"Put that gun up, Latimer, before you hurt someone," Sackett said in a taut voice.

"The only one who'll get hurt will be you if you don't dance," Latimer stated as he pointed the gun in Linc's direction.

"I wouldn't point that thing at me unless you truly plan on using it," Linc said as he moved slowly in the direction of his gun and gun belt that was hanging on a corral post.

"I plan on using it if you don't dance for me. I'll shoot you in both of your feet. Now start dancing," Latimer ordered.

"What's going on here," a voice from behind Latimer asked, causing him to turn around.

The voice belonged to the ranch foreman, Buck Benton. Latimer lowered the pistol as Benton moved up to where he was standing.

"He embarrassed me in front of all these men and it's payback time, Buck," Latimer stated as he stuck the pistol under his belt.

Benton looked towards Linc and said, "Come over here Sackett. What's the row all about?"

"I was riding that sorrel mare and had her near broke, but Latimer threw his hat under her when I rode past him and spooked her. I knocked him on his butt and he wants his revenge," Linc said as he walked to the corral railing where Benton and Latimer were standing.

"I'll not have a feud going on with two of my wranglers. It never stops with just the two. The next thing you know half the ranch hands won't talk to the other half and that's when real trouble begins. Latimer, you drop it. Sackett apologize to Latimer."

"I won't apologize until he does," Linc said. "I took a real pounding from that little mare and this fool undone a lot of what I'd accomplished."

"Latimer...you apologize to Sackett," Benton snapped.

"When hell freezes over," Latimer said with a frown.

"Apologize now, or hit the trail," Benton said seriously.

"It'll be the trail, because I ain't apologizing to this skunk," Latimer said, his eyes mere slits in his face.

"Go up to the house and ask Miss Shauna to give you your pay," Benton said evenly.

Latimer glared at Benton and then at Linc who had gotten near his gun belt by this time.

"Why you good for nothing...," he said and started to go for his gun.

Linc pulled his gun from its holster still resting on the fence post, fired and shot Latimer in the wrist, not wanting to kill the man. Latimer instantly grabbed his wounded wrist while the gun flew from his hand.

"Awgh, Latimer screamed out in pain. He cradled the bleeding wrist against his stomach and held the other hand over it. He looked at Linc with pure hatred in his eyes.

125

"You've crippled me for life, Sackett," Latimer screamed.

"You're alive, Jess; be thankful for that," Linc replied.

"You were going for me with that gun, weren't you," Benton said angrily.

"I don't take kindly to gettin' fired, Buck! Ugh..., oh, this hurts," Latimer said holding his wounded wrist and then going on. "I told you when I hired on here that I'd give you a full days worth of work and I've done that."

"Yeah, but you've bullied every man on this ranch with the exception of Sackett and me since you've been here. You're more trouble than you're worth," Benton said with a hard glare.

"You got what you had coming, Jess," Montana added. "Let it be."

"I'll go, but you can be sure you ain't heard the last of Jess Latimer. I'll be back and when I come, I won't be alone," Latimer said as he stumbled towards the ranch house and Miss Shauna.

"I've been looking for a good enough reason to fire that man; you gave it to me, Sackett," Benton said as they all watched Latimer stumble towards the house.

"I wouldn't have been so hard on him if that little mare hadn't given me such a workout," Linc said.

"You should have seen him, Buck," Montana said with a grin. "He rode that bronc for over two minutes of real 'gettin' with it' bucking. Why his nose was even bleeding by the time he got off her."

Ride the Hard Land

"Is that right, Sackett," Benton asked quizzically?

"That it is. She gave me the pounding of my life," Linc said honestly. "But she's a great horse," he then added.

"Why don't you go and wash up. You look a mess," Buck said with a slight grin. "I think you deserve to knock off a little early today."

"Hey, what about us, Buck...we had to watch him go through that beating," Stretch said with a grin.

"I'll give you some time off when you ride that little mare for over two minutes," Buck replied, getting a good laugh from the other wranglers.

Buck waited for Linc to crawl through the fence railing and head for the bunkhouse and walked up alongside him.

Linc looked at Buck knowing there was something Buck wanted to say to him.

"Keep an eye out for Latimer. I've heard from a couple of the ranches he's worked on that he carries a grudge longer than most men. And, he doesn't make idle threats," Buck said as they walked along.

"I figured as much. I've had run-ins with his kind before. Thanks for the warning, Buck; I appreciate it," Linc said with a slight grin.

"If I was you I wouldn't go out without my gun. One of the ranchers I talked to said they had a man ambushed while riding fence and although they couldn't prove it, they were pretty sure it was Latimer."

"Okay; I'll do that. By the way, are you going to the dance in Tombstone tomorrow night," Linc asked, hoping to change the subject?

"Yeah, I am. I'm taking Miss Shauna. She loves to dance," Buck said with a grin.

"I'll bet she's a real good dancer too," Linc said with a chuckle.

"None better that I know of," Buck said with a wink.

"I'll take your word for it, boss," Linc said with another chuckle.

"You'll have to because she only dances with me," Buck replied.

"Even at the dance, huh," Linc said getting another laugh from Buck.

"Yep, even at the dance," Buck said.

Chapter 18

BRIAN AND AJ had been on the trail five days when they finally reached Sundown. They headed to the place most male travelers headed upon entering a town; the nearest saloon. They were dry and needed something to cool them down.

They bellied up to the bar and ordered two beers each. The first one they downed in one long slug. The second one they took their time and enjoyed it to the fullest.

The bartender walked over to them and struck up a casual conversation.

"So, where are you from," he asked?

"Just out of Abilene," AJ said.

"I have a sister that lives in Tuscola," the bartender grinned.

"Oh, really... that's about thirty, thirty five miles from where we live," AJ replied.

The bartender looked at Brian and said, "You know, you look familiar to me. Have you been through here before?"

"Nope, I sure haven't," Brian said and gave AJ a quick look.

"You know another fella asked us that same question a couple of days ago. There must be someone running around with his face," AJ said motioning towards Brian.

"Must be at that; but I could swear I've seen you before...somewhere, if not here," the bartender continued.

"Were you in the War," Brian asked?

"No, I wasn't. I couldn't make up my mind which side to be on, so I stayed out of it all together," the bartender said truthfully.

"Oh, well this is my first visit to Sundown," Brian smiled.

"We hear you had a little excitement around here awhile back; something about the bank being robbed," AJ said, bringing the conversation to a subject they thought might give them a clue to Brent's whereabouts?

"We've had enough excitement to last this town a long time. We not only had a bank robbery, we had some yahoo shoot the sheriff and the doctor one day. He must have gone loco or something because he was a patient of the doctor's. When the sheriff went to wake him up and ask him some questions, he came up a shootin'," the bartender said.

Ride the Hard Land

Again Brian and AJ cast a quick glance towards each other. AJ took the lead, but was careful about asking too many questions.

"What do you know about the guy who did the shooting," AJ asked?

"At first we didn't know anything. The doc said the man had been wounded by the bank robbers when he and his wife met up with them.

"He wounded the sheriff and shot the doctor in the back and we didn't know for a few days if the doc was going to make it or not. Old Doc and the sheriff pulled through somehow, though. The doc gave us the man's name and description; it was Dan Burton according to the man's wife told the doctor," the bartender stated.

Brian gave AJ another quick glance and said, "Oh, the man was married, huh?"

"Yeah, a pretty little thing from what the doc said. The man was wounded by the bank robbers and the doctor thinks the sheriff waking him up caused him to think it was the holdup men come to finish him off."

"They didn't catch the guy," AJ cut in?

"Nope, they figure him and his wife are long gone by now. The sheriff's deputy...and brother-in-law...acted as sheriff until the sheriff recuperated and then was fired," the bartender said with a chuckle.

Just then someone entered the saloon behind them and the bartender looked towards the man. It was the sheriff, Gray Dawson.

"Say, Gray, we were just talking about you," the bartender called out to the sheriff.

When he did, AJ and Brian turned around to see who the bartender was talking to. When the sheriff got a good look at Brian's face he stopped dead in his tracks. Before Brian or AJ could even respond he pulled his pistol and aimed it at Brian's chest.

"One move out of you and I'll blow a hole clean through you," the sheriff snapped angrily.

"Whoa, Sheriff, what's this all about," Brian said holding out his hands in a defensive move.

"You know what this is about; you wounded me and damned near killed the doctor," the sheriff said as he held them at bay. "Take your guns out of those holsters with your opposite hand and real slow like lay them on the bar and then step away. The slightest move will be your last," he said coldly.

"Sheriff, I don't know what this is all about, but you've got the wrong man," Brian said as he and AJ followed the sheriff's orders.

"No...I don't think so. I looked you right in the face when I woke you up and you went to shootin', the sheriff said.

"We just rode into town no more than ten minutes ago, Sheriff," AJ started to say.

"You keep quiet; I'll do the talking here."

"This man," Brian said motioning towards the bartender, "said that a man the doctor had worked on shot you and the doc. I'd like the doctor to take a look at me and let him tell you if I was the one he worked on. He should know; the scar would be evidence wouldn't it," Brian said evenly.

Ride the Hard Land

"You're up to something; some kind of trick or something. You ain't fooling me with your innocent act," the sheriff said shaking his head.

"Look, put us in jail and have the doctor come over there and check me out," Brian said showing some agitation.

"Oh, I'll put you in jail all right...both of you," the sheriff said and then motioned towards AJ. "You, I'll hold to see if there're any wanted posters out on you. Let's take a little walk down the street to the jail."

Brian and AJ walked out of the saloon with the sheriff walking behind them carrying Brian's gun in his belt and holding AJ in his hand along with his own.

When they reached the jail he locked them both in the same cell, since the Sundown jail only had one cell. As he turned the key he backed up and grinned before saying, "There, I'd like to see you get away now."

"Go get the doctor, Sheriff," Brian urged. "He can straighten this whole thing out in just a few minutes."

"In due time, hoss, in due time," the sheriff snapped.

AJ had just about had all of this he could take and let the sheriff know as much.

"What is it about small towns that cause them hire the dumbest guy in town to act as their sheriff? My brother has told you how to handle this and you're too thick headed to see it."

"That'll be enough out of you. What're your names anyway," the sheriff asked?

"Sackett...I'm Brian and this is my brother AJ. We're from Abilene...the Texas Abilene, not the Kansas one," Brian said as he turned around and sat down on one of the two cots in the cell.

"If you're not too addle brained to know about telegraph machines you might try sending a telegram to the sheriff of Abilene and ask him if he knows the Sackett family. He'll tell you they own one of the biggest spreads in the area and that the sons of John Sackett are AJ and Brian," AJ said with a deep set frown.

"You know, I really had nothing to hold you on, but I think I'll let you cool your heels for a week or so and see if that takes a little of the sand out of you," the sheriff said with a frown as he glared at AJ.

Brian looked at AJ and grinned, "Good job, brother; a little bit more and you might get us both hanged."

AJ couldn't hold back a grin of his own as he said, "I hate stupidity, don't you."

Chapter
19

BRENT SACKETT STOOD looking out across the land that Julia and her dead husband had purchased. He shook his head and knelt down gingerly and picked up a handful of dirt. He let it run through his fingers for a second and then stood up and threw the remainder of the dirt aside.

"I'd rather ride the hard land than put my hand to farming," Brent said under his breath.

"What was that, Brent," Julia said as she walked up behind him?

"Nothing, I was just thinking out loud. I think what we'll do is head out for California in a few weeks. As soon as I'm strong enough to dig myself a grave in that hard ground out there, that is," Brent replied.

"Whereabouts in California do you want to settle," Julia asked?

"I was thinking San Francisco. I hear a man can make a good living out there. We can buy us a little place and drop out of sight. No one will ever find us out that way," Brent said thoughtfully.

"Tell me again what we'll do when we first get out to California," Julia said.

"We'll find us a preacher and get hitched. Then we'll go to the finest restaurant in town and have a big delicious dinner with wine, the whole works. Then we'll find the nicest hotel in town and make love all night long," Brent said as he put his arm around Julia's waist.

"You make it sound so wonderful, Brent. I can hardly wait until we get there. How long do you think it will take us to make the trip?"

"Not long at all, because we're going in style; by train. No long ride in a blasted covered wagon for us," Brent said with a smile.

"Do they have trains that go all the way out there," Julia asked with a puzzled look on her face?

"We'll take one as far as it goes and then go the rest of the way by stagecoach...how's that," Brent smiled?

Julia smile up at Brent and nodded her head, "I'll be glad when we can leave here. I worry every day that someone might come by and recognize you."

"I'm about ready to remedy that...today," Brent said seriously.

"Do you think you're up to digging in this hard ground?"

"Uh huh, I feel a lot better today. Don't worry your sweet little head over it; I'll take it nice and

Ride the Hard Land

slow. I don't want to re-injure myself," Brent said and looked off to his left.

He took on a serious look as he watched four men on horseback approaching. He'd seen a man ride by the place the day before and now four men coming from the direction of Sundown; it concerned him.

Julia noticed that Brent had tensed up and looked to see what he was looking at. When she saw the four men, she looked back at Brent.

"Get in the house, quick; I'll talk to them," she said.

Brent nodded, but kept watching the distant riders. The two of them hurried to the house and Brent went inside while Julia remained outside to meet the riders. Brent grabbed his pistol and held it by his side as he watched Julia through a small window.

When the riders arrived Julia greeted them in a friendly way. The four men rode up and stopped. It was the four Texas Rangers that Julia had seen in town earlier but didn't know who they were.

"Howdy Ma'am, the name's Culpepper. We're with the Texas Rangers and heard that someone around here might know something about the bank robbery that occurred in Sundown some time back.

"Your nearest neighbor back yonder said that you and your man had moved in here not long after the robbery and you might have seen something that could help us," Captain Culpepper said with a friendly smile.

"I'm sorry, sir; but we don't know a thing about the robbery. We arrived after it had happened. My husband is ailing and laid up so we haven't even been in to town for sometime," Julia said watching the ranger's eyes as well as casting quick glances at the other three men.

"Oh, is that right? I thought I saw a man with you as we were riding this way," Culpepper said suspiciously?

"Yes, you did; that was my husband. He walked out to get a breath of fresh air, but started feeling weak and went back into the house to lay down," Julia said as though it was the truth.

"I see. Well, if we could water our horses before we move on I sure would appreciate it," the captain said.

"Sure, help yourselves. The water trough is right over there by the corral. Would you all like a cup of coffee? I just made a fresh pot," Julia offered, hoping they would say no.

Culpepper looked at the others and then back at Julia, "I think we'd be much obliged, Ma'am. Thank you so much."

"You go ahead and water your horses and I'll bring it out to you," Julia said with a smile as she turned and headed for the house.

Culpepper watched her walk away and then commented to the others, "Nothing haywire here."

Ranger McNiece watched Julia walk away and shook his head slowly, "You know, that woman looks awful familiar to me."

"Oh, you think you've met her before, do you," the captain asked?

"Yeah, but I can't remember where. I think it was...," he paused as he searched his memory bank.

Ride the Hard Land

"No, I know I saw her. It was in a small town down south and three wagons rolled in; her and her husband were in the lead wagon. I even asked them where they were headed. I remember because she was so gall danged pretty," McNiece said.

"Where'd they say they were going," Culpepper asked?

"I think it was Sundown," McNiece replied.

"Well, they made it," the captain grinned.

The rangers rode over to the watering trough and began to water their mounts. Julia was busy pouring four cups of coffee and talking softly to Brent.

"I didn't want to act worried that they were here, Brent. I offered them coffee hoping they'd say no, but they wanted some," Julia said as she placed the cups on a small flat board to serve as a tray.

"They said they were Texas Rangers up here because of the bank robbery? Since when do the rangers send out four men to check something like that out? And then there was the two in town that you saw. It's usually just one ranger...but, six rangers total, huh uh; something's up," Brent said ponderingly.

"I'll get rid of them as soon as I can. I told them you were stove up and had gone outside to get some air, but started feeling weak again and had to go lay down. It'll be all right if you just stay out of sight," Julia said confidently.

"I'll be watching them through the crack in the door, so give 'em the coffee on the porch to give me a good view," Brent said.

Julia took the coffee outside on the porch and waited for the rangers to finish watering their animals. Once finished, the four men led their horses over to where Julia was waiting for them.

"Here ya' go," Julia said with a smile. "I've got some sugar for those who like sweetening, but no cream. Our cow up and died not long ago."

Ranger McNiece gave Julia another good looking over and then asked, "Didn't I meet you and your husband down around Brady awhile back?"

Julia tensed, "You may have. We moved up here from Round Rock and did pass through Brady."

"I thought so," McNiece said with a smile. "I remember your husband was a brusque kind of man. I know he wasn't too interested in talking to a Texas Ranger," McNiece said with a chuckle.

Julia thought quickly, "Oh, that wasn't my husband; that was his brother. No, I remember now, my husband had been driving their wagon because he could better handle the team his brother had just bought," she lied.

"Oh..., I could have sworn he said you were his wife," McNiece said with a frown?

"Nope, that I'm sure of; my husband is right inside if you want to meet him," she said, her words causing Brent to cringe.

140

Ride the Hard Land

"No, no, not if he's ailing. I don't want to catch something he might be giving off," McNiece said holding his hands away from him.

The rangers made small talk until they had finished their coffee. Captain Culpepper placed the cup on the flat board that Julia had used as a serving tray and then placed on a small table.

"Thank you so much for the coffee, Ma'am; and our mounts thank you for the water," he said with a slight smile. "We'll be moving along. Tell your man that we hope he gets to feeling better."

Julia smiled and said, "I'll do that. I hope you find the ones you're looking for."

She watched as the four men mounted up and started to leave. Suddenly she thought of what Brent had said about so many Texas Rangers riding together and asked, "Isn't it unusual for four rangers to be riding together? And, I met two more rangers in town the other day."

Captain Culpepper grinned as he answered, "Not when you're after the Black Jack Haggerty gang. It may have only been two men who robbed the Sundown bank, but you can be sure there are more gang members around somewhere."

"Oh, I see," Julia said and waved goodbye again.

Raymond D. Mason

Chapter 20

THE DOCTOR stood outside the jail cell with his mouth agape as he stared at Brian. No one said anything for a several seconds.

Finally the doctor said, "You look exactly like the man I tended to; but with one exception. He had a small scar on the side of his neck and you don't."

"If you'd like to check the area where you cut on him, Doc, feel free. I want you to tell this sheriff that I'm not the man who shot you," Brian said evenly, casting a quick glance at the sheriff.

"I don't have to, but if you'll raise your shirt the sheriff can see for himself that you're not the man," the doctor replied.

Without a word Brian raised his shirt so the doctor could see he didn't have a freshly made scar. The sheriff slowly moved to the jail cell and unlocked the door.

Raymond D. Mason

Brian and AJ grabbed their hats and walked out. AJ cast a hard look at the sheriff who quickly looked away. Brian shook the doctor's hand and walked past the sheriff without a glance.

The two brothers stood before the sheriff's desk and waited for him to return their belongings; that being their guns and money. When AJ received his billfold he opened it and counted the money with the sheriff looking on.

"It's all there," the sheriff snapped.

"Just making sure," AJ replied and continued to count.

"You don't know where this fella, Dan Burton is now I take it," Brian asked the doctor?

"No, I sure don't. You know that's a funny thing...his name that is. His wife called him Dan at one point and another time she called him Brent. I wasn't sure if she called him by his first and middle names from time to time, or if it was mistake on her part."

"She called him Brent, huh," Brian said quickly?

"Yes, I'm sure that's what she said. I do remember his last name as being Burton, though."

"And you say they were traveling by wagon?"

"Yes, but there was a saddle horse tied to the back of it," the doctor stated!

"Why are you so interested in this couple," the sheriff asked curiously?

"Wouldn't you be if there was someone running around that looked exactly like you," Brian snapped quickly?

"Yeah, I guess so," the sheriff replied.

Ride the Hard Land

"I'd pity that poor man," AJ said getting a glare from the sheriff.

The sheriff turned back towards his desk to sit down, but thought of something someone had told him the day before. He turned back towards the others with a questioning look on his face. Brian noticed.

"Did you want to say something, Sheriff," Brian asked?

"You know...George Beckman; he drives for the freight office here in Sundown; he told me that someone had moved into the Franklin place. He said he passed by there the other day and someone was cooking dinner.

"I knew the Franklin's sold their place, but didn't know if the folks had moved in yet or not. Usually new folks in the area come in and get acquainted with some of the local merchants, at least.

"If you'd like I can give you directions out to the place. I might take a ride out there and introduce myself to them; not that they are in my jurisdiction, law wise," the sheriff said.

Brian looked at AJ, "I think that would be a good idea, don't you AJ?"

"Yeah, it's something to do, anyway."

The sheriff drew them a map and handed it to Brian. They said 'so long' and went to the back of the sheriff's office to a small corral where the sheriff kept his horse and had put theirs to get them off the street.

The ride out to the Franklin place didn't take them very long since it was only four miles out of town. When they rode up Julia was in the back of the house cleaning and Brent was asleep.

They climbed down off their mounts and tied them to a small hitching rail. They walked up onto the porch and knocked on the door. It took Julia a few seconds to get to the door. When she opened it a stunned look came to her face as she quickly looked from Brian towards the bed where Brent was sound asleep.

Both Brian and AJ caught the stunned look and followed her eyes to the bed. They both grinned as Julia slowly backed away, allowing them to enter.

"Brent...," Julia said hesitantly, "...I think you have visitors."

Brent opened his eyes and eased his hand under his pillow where he kept his pistol while asleep. He sat up quickly and faced the door, the gun cocked and aimed at whoever it was that had entered.

When he saw Brian and AJ he looked as stunned as Julia had. He slowly lowered the gun and let the hammer down carefully. No one said a word for several seconds.

Finally Brian said, "Man, you are one hard man to track down."

"It must not be that hard to do; you found me," Brent said with the very slightest of smiles.

"Well, I'll be hanged," AJ said. "I thought Brian was out of his head when he said he'd met you down in San Antone. I guess I owe him an apology."

"I wouldn't, AJ, he is out of his head most of the time," Brent said, getting a chuckle from his two brothers.

"So who is this lovely lady," Brian asked, looking at Julia who was staring at him in disbelief.

"Oh, yes...Julia, I'd like you to meet two members of the Sackett family; the good looking one is AJ, the ugly one is Brian," Brent said with a more noticeable smile.

"Glad to make your acquaintance, Julia," the two said simultaneously.

"Likewise, to be sure," Julia said and then added. "I can't believe how much you and Brent look alike," she stated and then quickly added, "I'll put some coffee on and we've got some beef stew I can warm up; it's what we had for dinner," Julia said hurriedly.

"And what we'll have for supper tonight and breakfast tomorrow," Brent joked.

Brian and AJ laughed as they looked warmly at their long lost brother and his lady. Finally AJ said, "We'd like for you to come back to the ranch, Brent. The family needs you."

Julia had started to go back to the house, but stopped when she heard AJ's request.

Brent nodded slowly and said, "No, not with what I have hanging over my head. I've decided to leave Texas once and for all. Julia and I are heading out to California where we can get a fresh start; one without all the excess baggage I'm dragging around here."

"You could hide out on the ranch and we'd cover for you," Brian said.

"No, I don't want to 'hide out'; I want to be able to come and go as I please somewhere and not have to worry about some lawman identifying me. California will do just fine."

Brian cast a quick glance at AJ and said, "Ma and Pa sure would like to see you one more time before you leave for good."

Brent thought for a moment and then looked at Julia. He bit the inside of his lower lip as he contemplated the idea.

Finally he asked Julia, "What do you think, Julia? Should we make a detour through Abilene so you can meet the rest of my kin?"

"I'd like that," Julia said looking from Brent to Brian and AJ and then back at Brent.

Brent took a deep breath and slowly nodded his head yes. Another smile tugged gently at the corners of his mouth as he said, "Okay, whatever the little lady wants, that's what it will be. Abilene...here we come."

The End

Look for the next book in the Sackett series: Range War

See other series of books on following pages.

WESTERNS

The Sackett Series:

Across the Rio Grande
Three Days to Sundown
Ride the Hard Land
>Next in Series:
>Range War

The Quirt Adams Series:

The Long Ride Back
Return to Cutter's Creek
Ride the Hellfire Trail
Brimstone: End of the Trail
Night Riders
>Next in Series:
>Quirt Adams, Outlaw

The Ethan Brooks Series:

Beyond the Great Divide
>Next in Series:
>Three Desperate Men

The Luke Sanders Series

Day of the Rawhiders
>Next in Series:
>Moon Stalker

Raymond D. Mason

MYSTERIES

Nick Castle Series

Brotherhood of the Cobra
Beyond Missing
Suddenly, Murder
<u>Next in Series:</u>
The Cardiff Affair

Frank Corrigan Series

Corrigan
Shadows of Doubt
The Return of Booger Doyle
<u>Next in Series:</u>
An Invitation to Murder

Dan Wilder Series

A Walk on the 'Wilder' Side (Two stories in one book)
Send in the Clones
Murder on the Oregon Express
A Tale of Tri-Cities
Odor in the Court
<u>Next in Series:</u>
Irving Poole; Attorney at Large

Harley Quinn Series

A Motive for Murder
<u>Next in Series:</u>
Dark Nights, Bright Lights

Ride the Hard Land

Printed in Great Britain
by Amazon